What the critics are saying...

"OUT OF THE DARKNESS is an imaginative and tightly woven tale of two races establishing an uneasy peace to preserve their kind, and one woman's trip of self-discovery and sexual awareness. That the vampires and lycans in the story come off far more sympathetic and appealing than the humans is a testament to the Burtons' gift for characterization and story-telling." ~ *ParaNormal Romance Reviews*

"...Passion, hot eroticism and heartfelt emotion combine with mystery and intrigue to create a compelling, complex tale. For pure reading pleasure, don't miss OUT OF THE DARKNESS" ~ *Romance Reviews Today*

"Out of the Darkness is fabulous! This vivid glimpse of a world filled with vampires and lycans, secret plots and erotic sexual encounters will leave you clamoring for more. I love the characters in this story. Harlee seems to undergo a change, not just when she discovers her paranormal heritage but when she discovers her sexuality. This sexy, spunky gal gives these two men a run for their money and I enjoyed every moment of it. Duncan and Adrian are perfect for her, each giving her what she needs to become the woman that she is meant to be. Their explosive encounters will have you up all night reading. Each aspect of the story is well developed from the intriguing plot to the engaging secondary characters and let's not forget the extraordinarily erotic sex scenes. Regardless of what genre you enjoy - paranormal, suspense, erotic, you'll find it in this one...a definite keeper. I highly recommend Jaci and C.J. Burton's Out of the Darkness for everyone." ~ *Ecataromance Reviews*

OUT OF THE DARKNESS

Jaci Burton
C.J. Burton

ELLORA'S CAVE
ROMANTICA PUBLISHING

An Ellora's Cave Romantica Publication

www.ellorascave.com

Out of the Darkness

ISBN # 1419954180
ALL RIGHTS RESERVED.
Out of the Darkness Copyright© 2005 Jaci and CJ Burton
Edited by Briana St. James
Cover art by Syneca

Electronic book Publication October 2005
Trade paperback Publication March 2006
Excerpt from *Animal Instincts* Copyright © Jaci Burton 2005

Warning:

The following material contains graphic sexual content meant for mature readers. *Out of the Darkness* has been rated E–rotic by a minimum of three independent reviewers.

Ellora's Cave Publishing offers three levels of Romantica™ reading entertainment: S (S-ensuous), E (E-rotic), and X (X-treme).

S-*ensuous* love scenes are explicit and leave nothing to the imagination.

E-*rotic* love scenes are explicit, leave nothing to the imagination, and are high in volume per the overall word count. In addition, some E-rated titles might contain fantasy material that some readers find objectionable, such as bondage, submission, same sex encounters, forced seductions, and so forth. E-rated titles are the most graphic titles we carry; it is common, for instance, for an author to use words such as "fucking", "cock", "pussy", and such within their work of literature.

X-*treme* titles differ from E-rated titles only in plot premise and storyline execution. Unlike E-rated titles, stories designated with the letter X tend to contain controversial subject matter not for the faint of heart.

OUT OF THE DARKNESS

❦

Trademarks Acknowledgement

~

The authors acknowledge the trademarked status and trademark owners of the following wordmarks mentioned in this work of fiction:

Glock: Glock Inc.

Dedications

≈

From Jaci:

To the folks in Paradise – Thank you for always being there for me and for giving me a place to come to for coffee in the morning. I hope you find this one worth the wait. Thank you for your friendship and dedication. You are the best.

To the Breakfast Bitches…this wouldn't be any fun without the bitching. Love you babes and thank you for the sanity lifeline.

And to Charlie (the oh-so-talented CJ Burton)…for agreeing to do this again with me, for making it a crazy, sometimes hellish but always fun experience, just like our lives together. Hehehe. I love you, babe.

From CJ:

To my wife Jaci, who loves me with all her heart. I know this because we co-wrote this book, our second, and I'm still alive. Somehow despite juggling several projects, working a second job and attempting to potty train two new puppies, she managed to maintain a sense of humor and get the book done. You really have to love a woman like that…and I really do.

Prologue

ಬಿ

Stefan gasped for breath, the pain drawing him inside himself. It was too much to bear. He didn't have much time left. Blood poured from the wound in his heart, sizzling as it hit the carpet. It burned within him, the silver-dipped knife rapidly draining his life force.

What a fool he'd been. He should have known, should have suspected that his murderer would want him out of the way.

He crawled to his nightstand, wincing as his heart began to pound erratically against his rib cage. He fought to breathe, aware of the meaning of the soft gurgling bubbling up in his throat. Not much time left. Hurry!

He pushed the speed dial button on his cell phone, praying that Duncan would pick up. The sound of a Scottish brogue filled him with relief.

"Duncan," he gasped.

"What's wrong?" Duncan's worried voice sliced across the line.

His hands had gone numb. Using his last remaining strength, he gasped, "No time. Find Harlee...my daughter. She has to know. Go to Robert, he...he knows where."

"Harlee? Who the hell is Harlee? Stefan? Are you all right? Answer me!"

Collapsing, he was unable to summon the strength to hold the phone long enough to say any more, though he wished he could have revealed his killer. Damn. He prayed Duncan understood what he wanted, that Duncan would do what was necessary to find and protect Harlee. Numbness settled over his body, white light blinded him and the wrenching pain evaporated. A lifetime's remorse at having missed out on the pleasure of knowing his daughter washed over him.

You kept her safe, and that's all that mattered.

A soft voice called to him, despite the number of years since he'd last heard the sweet tones. Amelia appeared in front of him, a beautiful specter he'd waited a lifetime to see again. Her soft hair blew around her, teased by an unfelt breeze. She was still as breathtaking as the day he'd lost her twenty-five years ago.

Come to me, Stefan. I've missed you.

So many regrets, no time to atone for his mistakes. If only he could do things over again, this might have turned out differently. Then Amelia might not have died and Harlee would have grown up with them.

I love you, Amelia," he whispered as light filled his body. Suddenly all those regrets meant nothing and the past slipped away. He knew only euphoria now and an eagerness to be with his love. *Our daughter will be queen and you and I will be reunited.*

He gasped his last breath just as the door to his bedroom opened.

Chapter One

ဢ

Need slammed into Harlee's pussy, burning along her nerve endings and stabbing her womb, a sizzle of heated desire singeing her oversensitized nipples. Two pairs of hands and two mouths touched her everywhere as she breathed out a sigh of bliss. One's calloused palms caressed her distended nipples, pinching until she cried out. The taut buds tightened and sent ecstasy shooting straight between her legs. She ached all over, craved the touch of these two men like she'd never craved anything before. She needed them. Without them, she wasn't complete.

One lay underneath her, his thick cock nestled against her throbbing pussy. The other cupped her breasts in his huge hands, the crisp hairs of his chest tickling her back. He adjusted himself behind her, moving one hand away from her breasts to work the silky lubrication into her ass, stretching her until she burned with need, overcome with a hunger impossible to resist.

A needy whimper escaped her throat as the fingers left her slowly, only to be replaced by the broad head of his cock. She held her breath as pressure increased with each thick inch working its way into her tight back entrance, squeezing the shaft slowly entering it. Oh it burned, stretching her, filling her ass until she was on fire. It was exquisite, the pain, the tenderness he showed as he inched in slowly, drawing her hair to the side to lick her neck. She shivered, certain she had died and gone to heaven.

She wished she could make out their faces, but they were a blur, as if a fog deliberately kept their identities hidden. But she knew them, knew she was destined for this moment. And they adored her – their one goal was her pleasure. She felt like a queen, her body worshipped so completely it moved her to tears. She never thought she'd be loved like this.

The one under her grasped her hips in his powerful hands and positioned her over the flared head of his cock, tantalizing the entrance to her pussy by brushing against her clit. Spasms tightened her womb as he shifted, pulling her slowly down onto his shaft, impaling her with his thick heat. She cried out as her vaginal muscles tightened around his thick cock.

Both men filled her now, their cocks separated only by a thin membrane of skin. One thrust while the other retreated, each movement driving her clit against the pelvis of the one beneath her.

The world spun on its axis, shards of sweet ecstasy splintering inside her. The one behind her sank his teeth into the soft flesh of her shoulder. She whimpered as torturous pleasure pummeled her, taking her closer to the orgasm she so desperately sought.

She buried her fingernails in the chest of the one she straddled. He pulled her forward and took her mouth in a ravaging kiss that left her breathless.

This was ecstasy, the completion she'd spent her life looking for. She was close, so close to the edge of reason that she lost all focus. All she could do was savor each pulsing second as they took her higher and higher.

Pleasure burst and spiraled like a vortex inside her. She screamed, the keening wail more animal-like than human. Her climax washed over her, heating her body, boiling her blood. Her body was stretched on a torturous rack of pounding pleasure. They poured their semen into her, hot strikes of liquid filling her cunt and ass, sending her into another eruption even stronger than the first.

She couldn't take this. She was going to die from it. But oh, she never wanted it to stop.

The fog began to clear as her mind focused once again. She could almost make out the appearance of one of the men. Tanned skin, white teeth, sharp canines...

Sharp canines? She squinted, certain she'd imagined it, when a low growl from behind her made her half turn.

Surely that wasn't —

The hand clamping over her mouth took her instantly from dream to reality, from pleasure to mind-numbing panic. Gone was the dreamy, post-orgasmic euphoria, replaced by abject terror as strong hands pinned her to the bed.

"Shhh, no one's going to hurt you," a harsh male voice whispered.

Her heart thundered, swelling in her chest and mashing her lungs until she couldn't manage an inhalation. Her pulse rushed through her veins and she fought for breath as her throat suddenly constricted. When he yanked the covers off, her brain cells finally kicked in. She struggled, fighting against him with all she had. She'd been trained for hand-to-hand combat for God's sake...where the hell were her skills right now?

If only she could reach the gun in her nightstand. At least she had the advantage of knowing the layout of her bedroom. She pushed with all her might against the hands holding her, inching her fingers toward the nightstand drawer. But she was slammed back against the mattress and a hard body straddled her, driving the air back out of her lungs again. He used his body weight to keep her still and his hands to hold her arms above her head. She let out a shriek in hopes a neighbor would hear her, but a hand clamped down over her mouth again.

How many hands did this guy have? Dammit!

"Should we keep her mouth covered?"

That was a different voice than the first. There were two of them? How did they get in? She always locked the doors and windows and any breaking glass would have woken her since she was a light sleeper. She tried to make out their features but it was too dark. How the hell could they see when she couldn't?

She sent the command to her brain to move, but terror and the weight of the man sitting on her held her immobile.

Do something! Don't just lie there like a statue! Fight, dumbass, fight!

Brain cells once again engaged, she struggled, kicking upward and trying to scratch his hands with her fingernails, but it was like a fly trying to fight a bull elephant. He was simply too strong. And his weight on her diaphragm cut off her air, rendering her too weak to struggle.

She was *not* going to let this happen!

"I'm not going to take a chance on her waking the neighbors by screaming," the one sitting on her said.

"Ach. Then hurry," the other said. "Maybe we should blindfold her or knock her out."

Knock her out? Dammit, she couldn't let that happen.

"Blindfold. And gag. Find something to wrap around her eyes and mouth."

Frustrated tears stung her eyes and she blinked them back, trying to gather her wits. She was a trained government employee. She wasn't supposed to be in this position. And why the hell were these men here anyway?

She heard one of them rummaging through her dresser and in moments her eyes were blindfolded and something covered her mouth, making her gag. Nausea rose up, causing her stomach to convulse. She forced herself to calm down enough that she wouldn't throw up and choke to death.

No matter how hard she struggled, she couldn't fight off the sizeable man who abruptly hoisted her into his arms.

"Grab that blanket and cover her and let's get the hell out of here!"

She offered up a fervent prayer of thanks when the blanket was thrown over her naked body. At least she was covered now.

"Don't fight me or I swear I'll knock you out," the voice snapped. "We don't want to hurt you, but we have to get you out of here fast. You're in danger."

Danger? What the hell was he talking about? She was in no danger. Or she wasn't until these two broke into her house. They were trying to save her? From what? From whom?

This was all bullshit. And if he thought she'd lie compliant in his arms while he kidnapped her, then he was one can short of a six pack. She wriggled against him, arching her back and kicking out with her feet in the hopes he'd drop her and she could run. Because if he let her loose, she knew this area well and she could damn well outrun just about anyone.

If she just could get loose.

"Sonofabitch! It's like trying to hold a slippery eel in my arms!" he hissed to his companion. "Hurry the hell up and get the fucking door open."

Once out the front door, the one holding her sprinted, jostling her up and down and slamming her against his hard chest. His grip on her was like being bound in steel and despite her struggles, she couldn't budge. She heard the sound of a car door, and soon she was being pushed across cold leather seats and belted in. One of them slid next to her and held her still, wrapping one leg over hers and gripping her arms so she couldn't move. The doors shut, the engine fired to life and they peeled away.

Harlee shook so hard her teeth chattered. Nausea built in her stomach as adrenaline surged through her system. She couldn't throw up now. It was time to force her body to relax. She needed to think rationally and the only way to do that was with a clear head. She wasn't dead yet, so there was still a chance to escape unharmed.

Focus on your surroundings. You can't see, but you can still hear.

She tried to memorize each turn they made, but there were too many. She listened for any unusual sounds but the roar of blood in her ears blocked out anything but her own jackhammering heartbeat. Her mind was a jumbled mess of panic and what ifs, making it difficult to concentrate.

She lost track of time, of turns, unable to guess how long it had been since she'd been taken. It felt like hours had passed but she knew it hadn't been that long. Terror rose within her. The gag made her mouth dry, she was dying of thirst and even worse, she had to pee. Sweat poured off her body, no doubt due to the rush of adrenaline from being so harshly awakened and kidnapped. And her entire body trembled.

Why did they take her? Yes, she worked for the government, but she was only a psychiatrist. Was this about the vampires and lycans? Hell, no one outside the government knew they existed. Then again, maybe this had nothing to do with her work. But if not, then what?

God, none of this made any sense.

The only good thing out of all of this was that they hadn't hurt her yet.

Yet.

No, they'd covered her with a blanket and carried her out to the car. Other than holding her in place, gagging and blindfolding her, she was intact. She'd just have to wait and see what they had planned, but she wasn't about to sit back and let them call the shots. As soon as possible she'd make a run for it. She'd rather die trying to escape than suffer whatever they had in mind. And if it was about the lycan and vampire studies they'd done, she'd never reveal the location of the lab.

They were climbing. She felt the angle of the vehicle change as they started upward, her head falling against the headrest. She tried to imagine the parts of the area nearby that would have such steeply sloping hills but didn't know whether they had headed into the mountains or the city. Damn.

Being blindfolded and traveling in the backseat of a car while it wound around narrow roads was not helping her stomach at all. She tried to breathe slowly, but she was so damn sick she just knew she was going to toss her cookies any minute.

Finally, she heard the crunch of gravel and the vehicle slowed to a crawl, then stopped. This was her chance, maybe her one and only chance, to escape. When she heard the car door open and felt the seatbelt release, she tensed, waiting for her opportunity. When he reached for her legs, she pulled back and kicked hard. She heard the whooshing sound of indrawn breath, but God almighty it was like kicking stone! Her shins stung from the impact of pushing against his steely chest.

They grasped her ankles and jerked her across the seat. Taking a deep breath and fighting with all her might, she writhed against the hands that forced her from the car before she was once again lifted into arms so powerful that her pitiful fight made little impression.

A whirring engine sound grew louder, wind whipping her hair against her face. A chill bit into her skin and she shivered as one of them carried her closer to the roaring noise. She was placed inside a helicopter and strapped in, one of them holding her tight against him again, eliminating any chance of making a run for it.

Her stomach lurched as they lifted off. After it rose, she pitched backward as it flew at breakneck speed toward its destination.

Good God, had they mistaken her for someone else? Someone important? Who the hell would go to this much trouble to kidnap her?

After a quick, nauseating ride, the helicopter dipped then slowed, finally, *blissfully* landing. The loud whir grew softer and she was once again hoisted against a body too strong to fight. Not that it stopped her. He might be bigger and harder than her, but she'd make sure that whoever carried her had an unpleasant experience. She even managed her first smile since this entire episode started when she dug her elbow into his rib cage, rewarded with his groan and a curse.

Throughout the trek outside, then inside while riding on the elevator, she fought, kicked, growled and dug her fingernails into his hands until she drew blood. Tension made his muscles taut but he never said a word nor did he retaliate by striking her or hurting her in any way.

But dammit, she couldn't get free and she couldn't see! And her mouth was cottony from the stupid gag and she still had to go to the bathroom.

She heard a door open, then she was deposited none too gently onto a cold tile floor. The blindfold and gag were removed and she blinked rapidly, attempting to adjust her gaze to the brilliance of the lights. She squinted, lifting her hand to shield her eyes, only one thing on her mind at the moment.

"I have to pee."

Strong hands circled her upper arms and directed her to a closed door across the room. "There."

Disoriented, she worked her way toward the door. After blissfully relieving herself, she surveyed her surroundings, searching for an escape route.

Nothing. Not even a damn window in here. Were they in the basement? The elevator had risen, not descended, or at least she thought so. By the time they'd gotten on it her legs were shaking and her mind was occupied with emptying her bladder. She was way beyond the ground floor so no hope for escape from this room. She glared at herself in the mirror above the sink, forcing her brain to work. She was a government trained employee for God's sake...she had a decent working mind and had taken all the terrorism and capture classes. She'd even paid attention, though she doubted at the time she'd ever have to utilize the skills taught her. Surely she could figure a way out of here.

Dropping the lid down over the toilet, she sat and contemplated, racking her brain trying to remember everything she could from the brief glimpse she'd been given into the building she now occupied. The bathroom was across the hall from two huge double doors that led to...where? If she could slip out of here and make a mad dash for the door, maybe she could get lost and make her escape.

The element of surprise always worked in the movies and had been a critical part of her training. She'd wager they wouldn't expect her to run. Her best advantage right now was hoping they had underestimated her diminutive size, because she was a long-distance runner and could outpace just about anyone once she got going. If only she had clothes and shoes. Running barefoot and naked with only a blanket for clothing hindered her more than she cared to admit. But hell, she'd run into the nearest convenience store or pound on the nearest residence buck naked if it brought the police.

Ear pressed against the door, she listened for sounds of movements outside. Nothing. Squinting, she carefully turned the knob and pulled the door open an inch, quickly scanning the hall. No one stood between her and the front door. This was her chance. She tucked the blanket edges between her breasts, lifted it off the floor and tiptoed onto the tile, sucking in a deep breath.

She'd reached the handle and began to turn it when strong fingers clamped down around her wrist. Her gaze shot up to a pair of deep brown eyes as a man with salt-and-pepper hair shook his head.

"I don't think so," he said in slow, clipped tones, jerking her hand away from the handle and pulling her against his chest.

Goddamit! Her one and only chance to escape and she'd missed it. She blinked away the tears threatening to fall, refusing to show these people any weakness they could use against her.

They entered a room on the other side of the hall. Another man was in there. Broad, with brown hair and intense turquoise eyes that caught and held her gaze.

The one holding her nudged her toward the center of the room. She stumbled against the tail of the blanket but quickly caught her balance.

Okay, time to start figuring out how she'd get out of here. Deciding to encourage them to let down their guard, she moved to the fireplace and tried to calm the tension in her body enough that she wouldn't look like she was poised for flight. Let them think she was resigned to her predicament. As soon as they relaxed a bit, she'd get the hell out of here.

Wherever "here" was.

"What is this place?"

"You're at the Dark Moon headquarters."

"And what's that?" She'd never heard of it.

"It's the joint venture for the integration of vampire and werewolf nations."

Holy shit! Smack dab in the middle of enemy territory! And why the hell were they revealing their corporation name to her? Or their faces? Didn't they know who she worked for?

Confusion made her frown. Why tell her this, unless they planned to kill her now?

"Okay, none of this makes any sense. You wake me up, blindfold me, kidnap me then bring me here and tell me where I am? You're either the worst kidnappers in the world or you're going to kill me. And if you're going to kill me, why the hell didn't you do it at my house?"

"We're not going to kill you," the lean one said, looking at her as if she were an idiot. "And we blindfolded you to disorient you, to make it easier to subdue you."

"Not that you made it easy. And that's all you get to know right now," the other one said.

Some of that actually made sense. Not all of it, but some of it.

Harlee surveyed the area she could see, still confused but rather excited to be given an inside view of the vampire/lycan headquarters. The government had been after the whereabouts of these creatures for as long as she'd been working for them. The vampires and lycans were still a mystery to humans. A very dangerous mystery that her government intended to uncover, then eliminate. The stories she'd heard of the atrocities committed by these creatures made the hair on the nape of her neck prickle. Did she have anything to fear from them? Would they do to her what she'd heard they did to their captives?

Casting a wary eye around her, she became more determined than ever to find a way of escape. Though the man indicated they were in an office environment, this place looked like a home. The foyer was huge, the walls decorated with dark paneling, reflecting lights that were only marginally lit throughout the room. Expensive marble flooring decorated the foyer, leading her to believe that whoever lived in this house of horrors had some serious money. The whole place was huge if this library-sized room was any indication.

Heavy double doors led outside, but they were now guarded by two men who hadn't been present earlier. And if she thought the two in the room with her were imposing, they had nothing on the gargoyles dressed in dark camouflage guarding the doorway to her freedom.

"Who are you and why am I here?" she asked. Answers might help just a little.

"I'm Duncan," the broad one with the dark hair and blue eyes said, then added, inclining his head toward the older one, "He is Adrian."

"And?"

"And that's all we can tell you until Robert gets here," Adrian said.

Eyes narrowed, his expression hard and unyielding, Adrian obviously wasn't at all happy to be her babysitter right now.

She couldn't care less what he thought. "Let me go."

Adrian snorted. Duncan's lips curled into a half smile and they both crossed their arms over their chests, a silent "no fucking way" in response to her request.

Any other time she'd notice how tall they both were, how big, how…damned sexy and fucking hot they were. Okay, so she did notice it. She supposed even kidnappers could be good looking.

But were these two vampires? Or lycans? She'd met others. It was her job to psychoanalyze them, to use the government drugs on them in an effort to learn the whereabouts of their headquarters. But human drugs didn't work on lycans or vampires. Though she had medicated enough of them to get some really interesting insights into their physiology.

The main thing she'd learned over the past years about vampires and lycans was their inherent sensuality, their love of all things related to sex. Ruled by passion and desire, they fed on it, used it as part of their survival. They saw beauty and sensuality in everything, from art to literature to people. Things that the average human ignored, vampires and lycans found mesmerizing. Their senses were keen while the humans around them tuned out sights, sounds and scents.

Maybe that's why she'd always been fascinated by them, why she'd dreamed of them since her childhood, before she ever knew they existed.

The woman in her couldn't help but acknowledge that they were two of the most gorgeous men she'd ever laid eyes on. Testosterone filled the room, making it seem suddenly smaller and warmer. Duncan had very broad shoulders and large...everything. Big hands, tree trunk legs and shaggy brown hair. His blue eyes appeared kind, though obviously they didn't fit his personality since he'd just abducted her.

Then she turned her attention on Adrian. A couple inches shorter than Duncan, though still more than half a foot taller than her, he was leaner and definitely more mature. The silver intertwined with the black in his hair made him look wild and sexy and...what? Experienced, she supposed was the appropriate word. His dark brown eyes studied her like she was some unusual zoo exhibit.

"Sit down and relax," Adrian said, inclining his head toward the sofa.

She crossed her arms over her chest. "I don't remember a fucking invitation to tea," she sneered, her fists clenching in the blanket wrapped around her. "I need to get out of here."

They approached her slowly, cautiously, their bodies tense and expectant. She resisted the urge to back away. The last thing she'd show them was the fear threatening to turn her legs to jelly.

They both dressed in black. Leather. God, under normal circumstances a vision like that would make her mouth water. She forced a measure of strength to her voice. "Answers would be really nice as a start."

"How about a drink?" Duncan stepped to a bar across the room and poured a glass of water from a pitcher, handing it to her. She cupped the glass and drank greedily, trying to wash away the cotton in her mouth. Once she'd drained the glass, she cupped it tight in her hand, realizing that it could be used as a weapon if needed.

"Why am I here?"

"Everything will be explained to you once Robert gets here," Adrian answered in a cool tone.

His voice made her shiver, and not just from fear. Maybe it was the combination of pure sexuality dripping from his voice along with his penetrating eyes. She felt the husky tones vibrating in her pussy. It annoyed her that she could have such a physical reaction to a kidnapper who was either a vampire or lycan. She shook off the mesmerizing quality of his gaze and pulled the blanket tighter around herself. "Whatever it is you think you'll get from me, you're wrong. You might as well let me go."

"Not possible, lass," Duncan said.

There it was again. That hint of Scottish brogue she'd heard when he'd spoken in her bedroom.

"You're not safe there anymore."

Safe? What the hell was he talking about? "I was doing just fine until the two of you kidnapped me."

"We had our reasons," Adrian said.

Right. Like they could come up with any reasonable explanation for jerking her from her bed in the middle of the night, scaring her out of at least ten years of her life. She still couldn't fathom them knowing who she was. Deciding to play dumb, she said, "Then I'd sure as hell like to know what those reasons are. I'm nobody. I'm not important or a public figure. I have no money. I'm a psychiatrist and have nothing of value to offer. Why would you kidnap me?"

"More like a rescue, actually," Duncan said with a hint of a smile. Adrian followed up with a slight smirk.

Rescue? Now that made no sense at all. Her jaw clenched in anger. "I'm glad you both find this so amusing, but I don't know who you are, I don't understand why I'm here and I have absolutely no interest in hanging around to meet this Robert person."

The sound of pounding footsteps caused her to flinch, the awareness that the sound couldn't be caused by one person sending her heart racing. The more people who surrounded her, the less chance she'd have of escaping. She backed against the couch, bracing herself to bolt, gripping the glass tighter even though she knew it was useless as protection.

A half dozen men dressed in the same black combat gear as the goons at the door appeared at the foyer entrance, flanking either side of the wide doorway. Their dark eyes locked on her, suspicious gazes filling her with dread as she stared back in shock. Moving between them, a very tall, thin male entered the room. Long red hair flowed around the stark, savage features of his face as the floor-length black silk and brocade robe covered his body. He swept into the room with an air of authority and ownership, his gaze riveted on hers.

Adrian and Duncan bowed their heads and he nodded at them briefly before turning his attention back to her. His eyes widened for a second before his lips quirked in an amused smile. He turned to the men who'd come in before them and said, "Wait outside."

Tension filled the air before they turned and left, retreating like ghosts in the night to no doubt fill the nooks and crannies of this haunted castle with their scary blackened faces and battle gear.

He sat down on the sofa next to her. This was her chance. Gripping the glass tighter, she reared back, intending to crash it over his head. But he caught her wrist in a vise-like grip that belied his frail appearance. She winced at the pain shooting through her arm, but the pain was forgotten when he smiled at her and said, "Now you wouldn't want to hurt your uncle, would you, Harlee?"

The fight in her dissipated at his words and he released her wrist, prying the glass from her tension-filled fingers. She rubbed the spot where he'd gripped her. "What did you just say?"

"You look exactly like your mother."

She'd never seen him before in her life. Surely if her parents had known this man, she would have met him at some point. And she would have remembered him. "You knew my mother?"

He nodded. "Not the mother you know. Not the woman who raised you. That woman was not your real mother."

Confusion was now a normal state of being it seemed. She shook her head and swallowed past the tight lump in her throat. "What do you mean?

"Your mother was not Louise Parker."

Okay, this wasn't funny. "Yes, she was."

"No. Your mother was my sister Amelia. And you look exactly like her."

Who was this guy? And why was he lying to her? "I don't think so."

He watched her with cool detachment then reached for her hand. She jerked it away, deciding this man was some kind of crazy lunatic with an agenda she couldn't begin to fathom. Which only made the need to escape even stronger.

"Who the hell are you?"

"I am Robert, leader of the vampire clan. My sister Amelia fell in love with Stefan, leader of the lycans."

As a psychiatrist she understood the concept of brainwashing. If these people were in fact vampires and lycans, they were clearly trying to gain her cooperation by filling her mind with bullshit.

She *was* human. Her background and genetics had nothing to do with either the vampires or the lycans. She studied their species but only in order to find a way to break their silence, to help the government determine their whereabouts.

"You're lying. And that's the most ridiculous thing I've ever heard. My parents were Louise and Carl Parker and they were both human."

His smile was kind, but something cold lurked behind his icy gray eyes. "Yes, they were your *adoptive* parents. They were human. You are not. You are a unique race of half vampire, half lycan, and as far as we know, the only one of your kind. You are my niece and Stefan's daughter and within the last twenty-four hours you became the heir to the lycan throne."

Chapter Two

ဢ

Harlee stared, open mouthed, at this man who claimed he was the head of the vampire clan and her uncle.

A cold chill crept up her spine and she shivered, pulling the blanket tighter around her. It wasn't true. She had to remind herself that in war, captors would do anything to convince their prisoners to cooperate. "You can't really expect me to buy this. Surely I'd have realized by now if I wasn't human." The government had conducted an extensive background check on her prior to granting her high security clearance. No mention had ever been made of her being adopted.

Then again, court records were typically sealed. No! The whole idea was ridiculous and she felt stupid even pondering it. She *wasn't* adopted, that's why nothing was ever uncovered. If there had been anything, anything at all about her, the government would have uncovered it when they investigated her background.

Robert shrugged and examined one long fingernail. "Not necessarily. If you are not brought up knowing the species you were born into, there's no way you would have known. You would not exhibit any of the characteristics of either species, unless you were taught or forced to change. You have to be trained to use force of will to enact the change or an act of passion might trigger it."

"Act of passion?"

"Sex," Adrian interjected.

Her gaze shot toward the two men who'd taken her. Both of them stared back at her, their lips quirked in half smiles.

"Sex?" she repeated.

"Yes. Sex," Robert said. "Sex with a lycan or vampire. Since the government doesn't even acknowledge our existence, that would have been difficult. Although if you had murderous intentions, that could also bring about the changes within you. But we really don't know how any of this affects a hybrid such as yourself. It's never been done before, but we are fairly certain that tandem sex with one member of both species will bring about the changes."

She ignored his comment about sex with two men, the visual too uncomfortably familiar. Instead, she focused on the other words he'd used. *Hybrid. Different.* Like her other dreams, the ones she'd had since she was a child. She'd always thought she had a vivid imagination that had manifested itself in her strange dreams. She'd often dreamed of vampires and werewolves when she was little. Their world was so real to her it seemed as if she had grown up a part of it, which had seemed so strange to her since she'd never even known they existed until she went to work for the government. She'd always chalked it up to wanting to be unique, to wishing she had those special abilities that the mythical vampires and werewolves had. Their power, their sexuality, their ability to manipulate their environment in many different ways. As an adult, her childhood dreams of living with them had changed, becoming more erotic, kinkier than anything she'd ever done in real life.

Just like the one she'd been having tonight when they'd broken in and kidnapped her. Two men fucking her, licking her, biting her. She studied both of them now. They were so much like the men in her dream, though she hadn't been able to see their faces. But body size, hand size, they were pretty damned…

No! It *wasn't* them! She hadn't been dreaming of them, it had been two nameless, faceless humans. And a normal fantasy for a woman who hadn't had sex in too long to remember.

Living among vampires and lycans had been nothing more than childhood fantasy. She wasn't different and she sure as hell wasn't some hybrid. They had her confused with someone else. This was a mistake. Vampires and lycans weren't magical, sexual creatures. They were murderers and cannibals, preying upon humans and using them for their own twisted experiments. And now that she'd been led right to their headquarters, it was her duty to find a way to bring them down. "I don't believe any of this."

"You will," Robert said, his gray-eyed gaze capturing and holding her. She wanted to pull away but she couldn't. Something about him seemed so…God, she hated to even think it, but he seemed familiar. He pulled something from the pocket of his robe and handed it to her.

It was a picture of a woman with long red hair, green eyes and full lips. A smattering of freckles decorated the bridge of her nose and her cheeks. Harlee's blood chilled. It was like looking at a picture of herself. She looked up at Robert. "Where did you get this?"

"It's a picture of my sister when she was about your age."

The likeness was amazing. But not believable. They could have easily doctored any photo and passed it off as his "relative".

Placing the picture on the table in front of her, she stood, once again tucking the ends of her blanket around her. They hadn't mentioned her position in the government. Was it possible they really didn't know who she was? And if that was true, then did they really believe she was one of them? Deciding to use the advantage for as long as she could, she said, "My parents never said anything about adopting me." And how convenient that her parents were both dead and she couldn't ask them. She had no other relatives. She was supposed to trust these animals, act on blind faith after they yanked her from the safety of her home in the dead of night? No way.

"They were instructed not to. That was the condition we placed upon the adoption."

"Why did your sister and my...supposed 'father' give me up?"

Robert frowned and she saw pain cross his features before he quickly masked it. Another act for her benefit, no doubt.

"Relational fraternization between vampires and lycans was forbidden. Wars had been fought between us for less than one species taking up with another. It was against our laws. But Amelia and Stefan fell in love anyway, and no one ever knew. He spirited her away, kept her in hiding when they discovered she was pregnant. They were planning to come out after you were born and fight to change the laws. They figured two prominent members of the lycan and vampire clans would be protected, that their child would be spared from elimination because of her royal blood. They thought your existence would change everything."

"But?"

Robert inhaled sharply, his exhale sounding like a mournful sigh. "My sister died giving birth to you."

How could that be? The recuperative powers of their species were phenomenal. Now she knew they were full of shit. If they were even vampires and lycans. They hadn't yet proved that to her.

"Aren't you people like superhuman or something?" she asked, trying to play dumb. She wasn't supposed to know they even existed.

Robert cast her an indulgent smile. "Even our powers are no match for extreme blood loss. I don't know exactly what happened, only that she bled and she bled too fast for Stefan to bring help. Offering his blood wouldn't have saved her because he wasn't the same species. He could only hold her and watch her die, then he made a promise to her that no harm would ever come to you."

Why did that knowledge hurt? She had no idea who this Amelia was or for that matter who this Robert person really was. Yet his pain was real. She felt it, saw it in his grief-stricken eyes. It stabbed her with a searing ache, shocking the hell out of her. Human or vampire or lycan, he had suffered a great loss, one that obviously still plagued him. "I'm sorry," she said.

He nodded and inhaled sharply, then relaxed his shoulders. "After Amelia died, Stefan sought me out and told me what had happened. Both the vampire and lycan clans thought she had simply run off with a werewolf, defying our laws and traditions. We had no idea she had fallen in love with leader of the lycans, or that she had given birth."

"So why didn't Stefan take me in and raise me?" She realized that playing along with him gave her a distinct advantage, one she planned to use for as long as she could. Hope began to surface. These people really believed she was one of them!

He took her hand. She expected it to be cold as ice, but it was warm and comforting. "You have to understand that twenty-five years ago, the lycans and vampires were at each others' throats, literally and figuratively. A child born of a union between a werewolf and vampire would have been nothing more than a bargaining chip, a prize coveted by both sides. If Stefan had announced Amelia's death and your birth, the only result would have been anger, recriminations, chaos and either a tug-of-war to possess you or a fight to eliminate you. Stefan did what he thought was best for you. He hid you away, though it pained him greatly to do so. He loved you because you were his child and his only link to Amelia. I wanted you too, as the only part of my sister left. By the time he and I argued and nearly came to blows, we both realized the best thing to do to keep you safe was allow you to be raised by humans."

Oh, man, this guy was either a great actor or this was the most fortuitous case of mistaken identity ever. Either way, she was going to play the cards she'd been dealt.

"Okay, so that I understand. You wanted me raised by humans and kept away from both the lycans and vampires. And I was. If what you say is true, if I needed some catalyst to change, then I might not have ever known. So why the middle of the night kidnapping? Why not just let me be?" She shot a glare at Adrian and Duncan, neither of whom had the decency to look one bit chastised. In fact, Adrian arched a brow and Duncan smirked.

"Stefan was murdered last night."

The head of the lycans had been assassinated? Holy shit! She was dying to run to a phone and call her superiors. "Murdered? Why? By whom?"

"We don't know why or by whom. Stefan contacted Duncan right before he died and instructed Duncan to come to me so I could retrieve you and keep you safe."

A fine mist of doubt crept into her thought process. This story was way too out there to be false. This stuff actually happened! Oh, she didn't believe the part where they claimed she was one of them, but obviously there was a huge problem in the vampire and lycan world. And that could be a very good thing.

"So you're lycan," she said, looking at Duncan.

Duncan nodded.

"And you're?" she asked, looking at Adrian.

"Adrian is a vampire. And they will both protect you. With Stefan assassinated, we don't know who they're after next. We felt it necessary to retrieve you, not knowing if your secret was out as well. A risky move, but one we were willing to take."

"If no one knew about me, how could they know where to find me?"

"If Stefan felt you were compromised, that means even without your physical whereabouts, chances were one of our kind would find you. The secret is out now and we don't yet know what that means to either of our people," Duncan explained.

"That's true," Robert said. "Duncan came to me as Stefan requested and told me what happened. I instructed him and Adrian to bring you here, where you could be guarded until we figure out who killed Stefan."

She bent her head and rubbed her temples, a sharp headache forming. This was all too much to process. They thought she was a half-breed lycan and vampire, as far as they knew the first of her kind. As the niece of the vampire leader and the heir to the lycans, whoever this person was would wield considerable power.

As a government employee, she'd been given the required training. But it wasn't nearly enough. She was in way over her head on this and didn't have the background or the experience to play this game undercover.

But what other choice did she have? She was the closest human to ever get into the hidden vampire/lycan holdings. How could she not do her job to the best of her ability?

Fear and doubt mixed with a rush of adrenaline that had her limbs trembling. Forcing calm, she looked up at Robert, hoping he'd read the confusion on her face as shock at his revelation and nothing more.

"I know this is a lot to take in at one time," Robert said.

"That's an understatement," she mumbled. "I still don't believe any of this."

"You will," Robert said, standing. "As soon as you undergo the physical changes, it will all make sense."

Her head shot up. "Physical changes? How will that happen?"

Robert shrugged. "Easiest and quickest way possible. You're to have sex with Duncan and Adrian. Engaging in mating with a vampire and lycan of royal descent will enact the physiological changes necessary."

Her gaze shot to Duncan and Adrian. Sex? With them? With both of them? Whoa. No way was that in her job description. Besides the fact she would be screwed when they found out she wasn't who they thought she was, she'd also be…well…screwed.

Why did the thought of fucking a vampire and lycan not carry the obligatory revulsion it should? Heat shot to her pussy, moistening her. Her breasts ached and her nipples hardened. What the hell?

"Adrian, Duncan, see that the mating occurs quickly. Understandably, Harlee still has her doubts and it's up to the two of you to help her see more clearly."

They nodded and Robert headed toward the doorway. "Adrian and Duncan will answer any other questions you have. And I'll be in touch very soon."

Her eyes widened and she stood, hurrying after him and nearly tripping over the trail of the blanket. No fucking way was he going to leave her alone with those two. "Wait a minute! You're leaving?"

"Yes. I have to do things at my end. I need to find out who killed Stefan. The balance of peace between the lycans and vampires depends on it, as does your life. It has taken us many years to achieve harmony between us. With the humans breathing down our necks and trying to force us out of hiding, it's imperative that the lycans and vampires keep our agreement intact."

"But I can't stay here! I have a job, deadlines, a life! I don't even have any clothes." And she couldn't fuck these two men, no matter what her body thought! As soon as they discovered she wasn't one of them, she was dead.

Robert took her hand and held it between both of his. "One step at a time, Harlee. Right now it's important you're safe. I have already arranged to have clothing brought to you, and anything else you need you can ask Adrian and Duncan. There is so much more you need to learn, and I have asked them to explain it all to you. They and a handful of my people will be the only ones entrusted to care for you."

Oh shit, oh shit, oh shit. She had to do something to stop this! "I don't believe any of this. I will not let them touch me. I don't even know them!"

Robert patted her hand. "The thirst lies deep within you, Harlee. The more exposure you have to your own kind, the more you will want what only they can give you. Trust your instincts. Listen to what your body tells you. Soon you will not be able to resist. It is imperative that we know where you will spend your life. As far as which side is dominant, only time will tell. I will check in soon."

He kissed her hand and turned away, departing the room with the guards trailing behind him.

She stared at the doorway for a few seconds, trying to put her mind around all she'd been told. Panic made her fight for rhythmic breathing. She wanted to curl up in a ball and shut out all that had happened, but she knew she couldn't.

There was a job to be done and she'd have to do it. Which meant she had to think on her feet every second. Not only did she have to find a way out, while doing so she had to fend off the advances of two men who could easily overpower her physically.

In order to do that, she needed to face them on equal ground, and there was one thing necessary to do that. Right now she stood at a disadvantage, and she wasn't about to take another step until the problem was rectified.

She turned to them, hoping they couldn't see her tremble.

"I need some clothes."

Adrian thought she looked pretty damn good wrapped up only in the blanket, or even better, without it. His balls tightened in memory of the moment he'd crept into her room and pulled back the covers, revealing a body he saw clearly despite the complete darkness. Full breasts, coral-tipped nipples just begging for his teeth to tug at them.

He felt a pull of his own at the crotch of his pants and shifted uncomfortably, tamping down urges that made him want to rip the blanket from the redheaded beauty and sink his shaft into her quivering pussy. He knew the rules. Now was not the time. It had to be her choice.

"Someone will see to clothes for you in the morning."

She arched a brow. "It's already morning and I need something to wear. I can't feel my fingers anymore from clutching the stupid blanket."

His first thought was to tell her to quit clutching, but from the irritated look she shot his way he figured she wouldn't find it all amusing. Then again, he didn't see anything funny about this entire situation. This debacle, starting with Stefan's death and the revelation that Amelia had a daughter, could be detrimental to everything he'd worked for in the past years.

She looked so much like her mother it was uncanny. Long, flowing red hair, brilliant emerald eyes and a full, sensual mouth that was created to suck a man's cock. Hot dark visions of capturing that mouth and tasting her caused a roaring erection he didn't bother to hide anymore. Why should he? If she was going to acclimate to living in the vampire and lycan worlds, she'd damn well better get used to open eroticism. Their lifestyles weren't at all like the humans, who hid behind cloaks of propriety and denied their base urges.

He'd never denied a base urge before and wasn't about to now. And the way her gaze drifted toward the crotch of his pants told him a lot more about Harlee's libido than she would likely ever admit. His lips curled into a feral smile and he inhaled, smelling her blood and her arousal, so evident on the air.

Shooting a look at Duncan, he knew the lycan scented her too.

"Get her something to wear, Adrian," Duncan said. "She can't very well wander around in a damned blanket."

Why not? With a shrug, Adrian left the room, returning in a few minutes with the first thing he'd grabbed from his room. He tossed his T-shirt in her direction, which she adeptly caught with the one hand that didn't have a death grip on her blanket.

"This is the best you can do?" she asked, casting a dubious glance at the shirt.

"For now, yes. It's either that or the blanket, babe."

Rolling her eyes, she strolled to the bathroom. He couldn't help but turn around and watch the way the blanket molded to the full curves of her ass. When he looked at Duncan, his gaze was riveted in the same place.

Adrian shook his head. "She's trouble."

Duncan nodded. "Aye, that she is. But one hot package of trouble."

That's what he was afraid of. And he had no time for someone who could cause more trouble than she was worth. The situation between the vampires and lycans had been tenuous for years. The human government had already captured more of their kind than was comfortable and they couldn't rescue their own people. It was assumed the government was using their own people to try and find out the whereabouts of the lycan and vampire headquarters, or maybe even to conduct experiments on them. Hell, who knew what the humans were doing to them. Either way, it was bad. It was only a matter of time before they figured it all out and came after them. Which meant the ties between the lycans and vampires had to remain strong. One false move and the relationship they'd spent decades forging could be lost. "We don't need this right now."

Duncan turned to him. "We have no choice. I swore to Stefan to protect his daughter. You will do the same for her. We will do what is asked of us."

Yes, he would, but he didn't have to like it. And he didn't have to like his attraction to her. There were plenty of women to fuck. He didn't need this one. His life was complicated enough.

"Holy hell."

Adrian looked up at Duncan's comment. Harlee stood at the entrance to the room, his worn black T-shirt skimming her thighs, revealing long, slender legs. Even though the shirt was miles too big for her, her full breasts and hard nipples were clearly outlined against the threadbare cotton.

He should have grabbed a thick coat instead.

"I'm hungry," she announced.

So was he. Painfully hungry, and in a way that surprised him. He hadn't had such a ferocious need to mate in a very long time. Fucking was lazy, women were easily available but he never felt the feral, desperate mating need so many of his people had.

Until now.

"I'll fix us some breakfast," Duncan said.

Her eyes widened. "You cook?"

Duncan grinned. "Of course. I have to eat, lass. I come from a family of thirteen brothers. If I wanted to eat and my mother wasn't fixing anything at the time, I had to learn to cook. We all did."

"Well surprise, surprise." She shot a look at Adrian. "And what are *you* good at?"

Adrian let his lips curl ever so slightly upward but didn't respond. She snorted and quickly turned away.

Oh yeah. She knew what he meant. Let her think on that one for a bit. The sooner he fucked her, the sooner he'd get her out of his life so he could get back to his real job.

"So, do you two work together?" she asked.

Duncan kept his back to her while he cooked. Adrian set the table and Harlee sat her ass down in one of the chairs like a queen waiting to be served. He slid into a chair next to her.

"In a way, yes," Duncan said. "I'm head of lycan security. Adrian does the same for the vampires. We frequently cross paths, especially when there's a meeting between the two clans or issues with the humans."

Duncan set a cup of steaming coffee in front of Harlee. She piled on the cream and sugar until it looked more like milk than coffee. "What kind of meetings? And thank you for the coffee. I'm a real bitch without it."

"So that explains it," Adrian said.

"Funny," she replied. "Tell me about your meetings."

"The meetings are none of your business," Adrian said. Robert said to explain "things" to her. Since he wasn't specific about which things to explain, Adrian decided to treat her like any other outsider. She'd only get the information he decided to give her.

Hell, for all he knew she'd want to go running to her human government and turn them in. Damn Robert for putting them in this precarious situation. She might be kin, but it hadn't yet been determined if she could be trusted. Blind faith could get them all killed.

"I thought I was part of the higher-ups in your world," she sniffed. "Shouldn't I be told everything?"

"Babe, you aren't shit right now, so you might as well lose the delusions of grandeur." She was probably an ex-cheerleader or prom queen, totally spoiled by her adoptive parents into thinking she was entitled to whatever she wanted.

"I have no delusions. I'm just trying to figure out where I am in the family tree of both clans." Her brows knit in a tight frown. "Thanks for being so welcoming. It makes me feel all warm and fuzzy inside."

Duncan snorted at her sarcasm.

If she thought to shame him, she was working on the wrong guy. "I'm here to protect you, not become your best pal. And if you're looking for a tour guide around the hierarchy, you'll have to find someone else. That's not my job."

"Is he always this friendly?" she asked Duncan as he served their breakfast.

"Usually," Duncan replied with a wink.

They ate in silence. Obviously being kidnapped and having her life turned upside down hadn't affected Harlee's appetite. She wolfed down her plate of food like she hadn't eaten in a week. Three cups of coffee and two helpings later, she pushed back from the table with a satisfied sigh.

"Lass, where do you put all that food?" Duncan asked. "Your body is thin as a rail. I was expecting you to pick."

"Nervous energy," she replied, standing and taking her plate to the sink. "And I run and lift weights. I burn a lot of it off."

Adrian wondered what other outlets she had for her nervous energy. He had a few ideas on that but doubted she'd be interested in hearing them. Then again, he'd find out soon enough.

The idea of sinking his cock into her hot pussy wasn't at all unpleasant. Her scent already made him hard. Her sensuality, though she tried to hide it, was obvious. She'd be a wildcat in bed. That part of the job wouldn't be a hardship at all.

When she cleared off the table and washed all the dishes, he had to admit he might have had her pegged wrong. Or at least the part about her being a princess who expected to be waited on.

The rest of her he'd have to withhold judgment on. But he'd be watching Harlee very closely. Despite her uncanny resemblance to Amelia, he still didn't trust her. After all, she'd been raised as a human, and though most humans weren't even aware of their existence, the government would be very interested in any human claiming to have seen the headquarters of the lycan and vampire clan. Of course they'd eliminate the witness immediately, but the end result would be the same.

She could bring an end to all of them with one phone call.

And no matter who she was, he'd never allow that to happen.

Chapter Three

ဆ

"I need a shower and some clothes," Harlee said. They'd eaten, cleaned the kitchen and she felt mostly naked traipsing around in nothing but a T-shirt, which left her at a decided disadvantage.

Adrian rolled his eyes. "Can't you do all that in the morning?"

"In case you haven't noticed, slick, it *is* morning. Or at least I think so since there aren't any freaking windows here at the bat cave."

"She's right," Duncan said. "It's six in the morning."

Harlee leveled an "I told you so" smirk at Adrian. "Shower? Clothes?"

"Fine. Follow me."

Adrian led her out of the kitchen and down a long hallway toward a carpeted staircase. Her bare feet sank into the plush carpet over each step, her hand gliding over the cherry wood banister that gleamed as if it were polished daily.

At the top of the stairs was a sitting room. She could barely make out the antique furnishings since the hall was only dimly lit.

"Bet y'all miss sunrise, don't you?" she asked, glaring at Adrian's back.

"Sunlight's just fine for me," Duncan said. "I'm a lycan."

Adrian stayed silent while they walked down a long hallway flanked by at least six rooms on either side. He chose the one at the far end of the hall on the right, opening it and

Even a completely heterosexual woman such as herself would have to think "wow" when looking at her.

"Hey there," the woman said, her face lighting up with a welcoming smile. "We all just heard about you. Wow, bet it was as big a surprise for you as it was for us, huh?"

"Who are you?"

"Oh. Sorry." She approached and grasped Harlee's hand, shaking it vigorously. "I'm Annmarie. Adrian's cousin. Well, really distant cousin, actually, but hell, with us vampires we're all related by bloodline in one way or another. Robert told me you needed some clothes and figured we were close enough to the same size so I brought you a few things to wear."

Adrian's cousin? Interesting. Annmarie was much more outgoing and friendly than Adrian. "So you're a vampire too?"

Annmarie grinned. "Well I hope so since at least half the folks in the place are."

"The other half being werewolves," Harlee finished for her.

"Right. And you're a bit of both." She grinned again. "That's wicked."

No, it was bullshit, but she played along. "I don't know about that. It's just confusing as hell to me."

"I can imagine. And I can't believe the only thing Adrian gave you to wear was his disgusting old T-shirt." Annmarie wrinkled her nose. "Take that thing off and try a few of these on."

Harlee followed Annmarie's pointing finger to the bed, where over a dozen outfits were laid out for her, along with bras and underwear. Only they weren't exactly the type of clothes Harlee typically wore.

Low-cut blue jeans, lots of leather, tiny little skirts and skimpy little tops just weren't her standard items of clothing. But apparently they were Annmarie's.

"Ummm…"

Annmarie grabbed her hand and dragged her to the bed. "Oh, come on. I can already tell you have a killer body. Let's show it off a little!"

"I don't typically wear…"

Annmarie rolled her eyes. "Puleez don't tell me you try to hide that made-for-sex body, honey. God, you'll have the lycans and vamps around here sprouting hard-ons night and day."

Not exactly what she was looking to do. In fact, hiding in her room until she could figure out how to escape sounded much better.

But Harlee quickly learned that Annmarie didn't take "no" for an answer. Before she knew it she was trussed up like a leather-clad woman in bondage in tight pants that fell way below her belly button. If she sat down she was certain the crack of her ass would be visible.

And the top was worse. A tight spandex midriff that bared her belly completely. When she looked at herself in the mirror, she couldn't believe it was really her. That vixen looking back at her couldn't possibly be the same woman who wore business suits to work and sweatpants with long T-shirts at home. No, it wasn't possible. Because the woman in the mirror looked hot and hungry for sex.

Annmarie insisted they comb out her hair and let it curl naturally, leaving it falling in soft waves to her shoulders. The tight bodice squeezed her breasts together, offering way too much cleavage.

She felt ridiculous.

She felt sexy. Wanton. Oh shit, she was in deep trouble.

"You look so fucking hot," Annmarie proclaimed. "You and me are going to have to do a night in the city sometime. We could do some serious damage to the male population together."

Harlee thought if she went anywhere in Annmarie's company she'd be pretty much invisible. The woman was gorgeous, vivacious and flirtatious. Everything Harlee wasn't. Oh she'd had her share of romantic entanglements, but she found sex to be way overrated and long-term relationships not worth her time.

"Christ, Annmarie, did you have to bring out your best 'fuck me' clothes?"

Harlee whirled at the sound of Adrian's voice. He stood in the doorway, one arm raised as he leaned against the frame. Duncan had already stepped into the room, his eyes wide.

"Nice," Duncan said, walking around Harlee then looking at Annmarie. "Well done."

"You would think so, stud," Annmarie said, lifting her finger to trail one blood-red nail under Duncan's chin. "She's hot, isn't she?"

"Hell yes," Duncan replied. "With you dressing her she has to look hot."

"I'll take that as a compliment, then," Annmarie said, winking at Duncan before moving away.

Adrian didn't say a word, just leaned against the door and stared at her, his brows knitting into a displeased frown.

Harlee heated from her toes to her face, no doubt blushing a very unbecoming crimson.

"Well?" Annmarie asked, crossing her arm and leveling a glare at Adrian.

"Well what?" he replied.

"How does she look?"

He pushed away from the door and sauntered in the room, stopping in front of her. "I'd do her."

Oh, God. There went the visuals again. And her body, heating this time not from embarrassment but from a sexual awakening that had really lousy timing. She never got turned on when men looked at her. Never. Why did the looks she got from Duncan and Adrian make her womb clench and her pussy quiver in anticipation?

"You're both practically drooling on her," Annmarie said with a note of glee in her voice. "Perfect!"

"For the love of blood, Annmarie. You're scaring the poor girl to death."

Harlee turned toward the doorway, her eyes widening as a woman walked in. She looked like a slightly older version of the woman in the photograph Robert had shown her earlier.

"She doesn't look scared to me," Adrian replied.

The woman waved her hand and stepped in front of Harlee. "Of course she's frightened. Dragged out of her bed in the middle of the night and then my brother drops a bomb of epic proportions on her. Who wouldn't freak out a bit?"

Okay, so this woman was Robert's sister? "I thought Robert said that his sister…"

The woman smiled, her hazel eyes filled with warmth. "Amelia was my older sister. I'm Sara, the youngest of our clan. And you are my niece." Sara's eyes filled with tears and squeezed Harlee's hands. "You look so much like her it's as if she's come back to life. Welcome to the family, darling."

When Sara enveloped her in a hug, Harlee closed her eyes, almost wishing she really was who they thought she was. But she wasn't. She was human and it was her job to see that all the people in this room were eventually taken in and destroyed.

Something about that thought jabbed at her, nausea rising rapidly. She pushed back and attempted a smile. "I'm happy to meet you, Sara."

"Surely we can find something more...appropriate for her to wear, couldn't we?" Sara said, glaring at Annmarie.

Annmarie's lips curled in a venomous smile. "She looks hot. Leave her alone. You're just jealous because you're fucking Adrian."

Harlee couldn't contain the shocked gasp. She looked at Sara, who still smiled warmly, then over at Adrian, who shrugged.

So he was having a sexual fling with Sara? Though very attractive, Sara didn't look at all Adrian's type. And that thought almost had her bursting out laughing. Just what kind of woman did she think was his type? As if she had any clue. Obviously his type was Sara, it wasn't any of her business and she had no right to feel the twinge of jealousy she felt.

"You're so crude sometimes, Annmarie."

"Oh please. Like you two haven't gotten it on in the middle of the hallway on some nights. Give it a rest, Sara, and quit trying to play sweet and innocent for Harlee's sake."

Sara's face contorted in anger, but she quickly hid it and linked her arm in Harlee's, once again offering a calm smile. "Some people have no class. Come, darling, let's go downstairs to the library and you can tell me all about yourself."

"I don't think so," Duncan said, blocking the doorway before Sara could lead her through it.

"Why not?"

"Because Adrian and I have things to do, and those things include Harlee. So you'll have to save your inquisition for later."

Things? What things? Oh, God, surely they weren't going to attempt to have sex with her right now, were they? She knew she shouldn't have put on these clothes. They made her look...available.

"Very well," Sara said, stepping away from Harlee. "We'll spend some time together later, dear."

"I guess that means I don't get to hang out either," Annmarie said, her full lips curving into a pout.

"Not right now," Adrian said.

"I'll catch you later then," Annmarie said, giving Harlee a quick hug. "Just relax, honey. I know this is all a shock to you, especially since you didn't even know our kind existed before last night, but we're really nice people. You'll see once you get to know us."

She would never get to know them. Any of them. Because she had to do her job. "I'll see you soon," she said, feeling strangely guilty for lying to Annmarie. She really wasn't very good at this covert operations stuff. Lying always made her sick to her stomach.

After Sara and Annmarie left, Harlee stood in the center of her bedroom, alone with Duncan and Adrian. Her mind and body tuned in to both of them, her traitorous libido flaming with anticipation. Her nipples puckered and she crossed her arms over her breasts to hide the evidence of her arousal.

"She's in heat," Duncan said, inhaling deeply. His nostrils flared out and his eyes half closed. "I can smell her. Hot, aroused, just like last night in her bedroom."

Heat singed her cheeks as she recalled the exact moment they woke her up. Right in the middle of an amazing orgasm and a dream about two men sandwiching her between them, driving their cocks into her pussy and ass. God help her she was on fire.

"I know," Adrian said. "Her blood boils deep within her, but she obviously hasn't yet learned to recognize the signs of heat."

"I'm not having sex with either of you," she blurted, panic making her mind go blank. She had to do something to stop this. Her body may want them, but she had to fight it and them or she'd be dead. If they fucked her and discovered she didn't change into either a lycan or a vampire, the ruse would be over and they'd kill her for sure.

"This is the only way to bring about the change," Duncan said, moving toward her. No more than an inch separated him from her as he came up to her side, his chest pushing forward and brushing her shoulder as he inhaled deeply. "You don't have the knowledge to force it and it's already obvious you're not going to fly into a murderous rage. So sex is the only way."

She shuddered as his lips made contact with her neck. "Ah, you smell so sweet, Harlee. I could give you much pleasure." He buried his nose against her neck. She stood, frozen, her body sizzling, her pussy moistening with desire.

"I could make you come with just a few flicks of my tongue on your clit," he whispered against her neck. "Then when I fucked you, the lycan within you would burst free. You could be wild, untamed as the animal within you comes to life."

Oh God. Her heart slammed against her ribs, her clit knotting and swelling as his words soaked her panties. She looked over at Adrian, who stood there and watched. His cock was hard, visible against the leather of his pants. Thick, long, it made her mouth water and she flicked her tongue over her lips to moisten them. The action made his eyes darken and he took a step toward her.

If he touched her too, if he used the same words Duncan used, she'd be lost. She had a tenuous hold on her self-control right now. She couldn't explain this unexpected desire, this need to strip them both down and let them do what they wanted to her and in turn explore every inch of their bodies with her hands and mouth. But she knew she had to stop it.

Remember what they told you vampires and lycans do to humans. The savagery, the animalistic behavior. It's your responsibility to put a stop to it. You're the only one who's ever gotten this far.

She closed her eyes and forced the pictures she'd seen into her mind. Pictures of humans lying dead, eviscerated, drained of blood, all because of what these creatures had done. A cold chill skittered down her spine and made her shiver. Duncan lifted his head and she opened her eyes.

"I need more time. I can't do this right now. It's all too much, too soon," she pleaded.

"Putting it off won't help," Adrian said, drawing close enough that she could smell his musky scent. It penetrated her senses and made her tremble with need. "It's in you. The thirst, the hunger, the lust, just waiting to be released."

"The sooner you allow it to happen, the sooner you'll feel more comfortable here," Duncan whispered.

"Please don't do this to me." She'd never begged for anything in her life, always felt she was strong enough to withstand anything. But this...this she couldn't handle. Not right now. Not ever.

Duncan took a step back.

The heat in Adrian's eyes smoldered. "We'll wait. For a while. But you know I'm right. I bet you've always felt something deep inside, sensed it in your dreams. You just didn't know what or why. Duncan and I both knew it the minute we entered your bedroom. We'll give you a little more time, but we're not going to wait forever. Besides, sometimes waiting is good. Builds the tension. But soon you're going to want us as much as we want you."

What were they doing to her? How could she loathe what they were, yet need them with a ferocity that shocked her? She had to find a way out and fast. But at least for the moment she had a reprieve.

Relief nearly made her fall to the ground. Her muscles were so tense her jaw ached. She forced calm into her system and smiled, trying to think of something to distract them from their primary "mission". "Thank you. I have so many questions that haven't been answered yet."

Duncan nodded. "Let's start in the library. We'll show you the books outlining the lineage of both the clans. It might help to know exactly where you are and to learn a bit more about us."

"That sounds wonderful. Shall we go?" *Get me out of this bedroom and away from thoughts of what I almost did.* Shame washed over her. How easily she'd let them manipulate her with whatever powers they had. No way would she respond to these creatures, knowing what they were capable of.

She had to get her head screwed on straight and keep it there. These people weren't human. They were savages. If it took every waking moment, she would keep reminding herself to fight the spell they'd cast over her.

Chapter Four

ॐ

The library was phenomenal. The first thing to catch her eye was the dark, rich red carpet spread like a sea of blood across the floor. How appropriate, Harlee thought.

Duncan and Adrian had taken her from the residence to the elevator and up to the corporate floors housing the operation known as Dark Moon. Apparently the lycan and vampire headquarters was also where many of the vampires lived, so corporate shared space with housing, with housing located underground and corporate aboveground. The building was located outside the city on several thousand acres of private land. Very secure, very private.

The library was filled with floor to ceiling bookshelves, antique Queen Anne furniture and glossy cherry wood tables, where they now sat with thick volumes of gold encrusted books spread open for her perusal.

What she wouldn't give for her PDA right now so she could make notes of everything she saw and heard. The lineage of both the vampires and the lycans was astounding, going back multiple centuries.

"So what you're telling me is that vampires and lycans have lived among humans for at least ten centuries?"

"As far as we can tell. The history books only go back so far," Duncan explained. "For so long much of our history wasn't documented for fear it would fall into the wrong hands."

"Human hands, you mean."

Duncan nodded. "The elders who started these volumes wrote as far back as they could recall, but it's estimated that we have been here since the time of Christ."

Her eyes widened. "Really?"

"It's not like the movies, Harlee," Duncan said with a smirk. "Actually, we're very similar to humans in a lot of ways."

Harlee choked back a snort. "How do you figure that?"

"We look the same, we run businesses, we raise families."

"You drink blood, you shapeshift into wolves..." she finished. "That's hardly the same as humans."

Duncan laughed. "Oh lass, you sound just like them. Humans are meat eaters, just as lycans are."

"Yeah, but we tend to avoid eating each other."

"Meat is meat. Granted, at first our people didn't discern, but eventually they figured out that eating humans not only called unwanted attention to themselves, but there were much tastier things to eat. Long ago, lycans stopped eating humans. Now, only the occasional rogue will do that."

"That's the freaking understatement of the year," she replied, shaking her head at their rationalizations. She wished she could reveal what she knew but then they'd know who she worked for, so she had to bite her lip and keep her mouth shut about the atrocities she'd seen photographs of. Atrocities committed by vampires and lycans. Instead she turned to Adrian. "What about blood?" Harlee asked. "Legend says you need it to survive."

Adrian nodded. "That's true to a certain extent. We eat food, just as you do. But we drink blood to heighten our senses and increase our strength."

"Human blood." Harlee fought back a shudder. How could she possibly be a hybrid of both species when the very thought of drinking blood or tearing flesh from bone made her nauseous?

"Not necessarily. While it's true that the blood of a human is the richest and enhances our powers the most, any blood will do, and just as Duncan said, vampires stopped doing humans, well, the unwilling ones anyway, long ago. And we never drink lycan blood. It makes us sick," he finished with a direct look at Duncan.

Duncan shrugged. "Good thing, too. There'd have been massacre otherwise. It's to your advantage that vampire hides are tougher than buffalo and taste like burned leather. Otherwise the lycans would have obliterated your species centuries ago."

"Kiss my ass, lycan. There's no way a bunch of Neanderthal wolves could defeat us," Adrian said.

"Up yours," Duncan replied.

Then they grinned at each other. Harlee rolled her eyes at both of them, wondering if testosterone was universal for all species. It had to be, since it appeared to be the key to men acting like idiots.

Listening to the two of them insulting each other made her laugh for the first time since she'd been there. Once again she found it difficult to reconcile these people with the information the government spouted about vampires and lycans.

"So if not from humans, where do you get your blood?" she asked Adrian.

"One of Dark Moon's enterprises is cattle ranching. Cattle blood is rich enough to enhance our powers. If we could only keep the lycans from hunting and eating them we'd have a copious food source."

"Hey now," Duncan objected. "Hunting and killing prey is ingrained. We can't help it. Besides, there's plenty of cattle to go around."

Admittedly, Harlee could sit and listen to both of them talk for hours. Not only was the information fascinating, but Duncan's Scottish brogue was like beautiful music, and Adrian's husky tones were like a caress on her skin. Her senses were in overload just from their voices. Before she started drooling, she turned away and focused on the volumes of history spread out on the table before her.

"So does the history give you any idea of your origins? Were you always here, were you once human and...mutated somehow or did you come from somewhere else?"

"Like outer space?" Adrian asked, an amused smirk on his face.

"Whatever. How the hell am I supposed to know? Yesterday I was a human who didn't even know your species existed except in horror movies and in books. Fiction, fantasy, not this bizarre reality you're forcing me to accept at face value, so cut me some slack." She lifted her chin, supremely satisfied that she'd pulled off a big lie like that without stumbling.

"There are a lot of species on this planet that even we don't know about," Duncan said. "It's only humans who are arrogant enough to think they are the master race here."

"Other species? Like what?" Nothing the government knew of, or at least none that her security clearance made her privy to.

"We don't know. We've read things in the history books that lead us to believe they exist. Maybe they've chosen to keep their identities a secret. Maybe we're the first guinea pigs with the humans," Adrian added.

"Guinea pigs?"

"Humans are the dominant population. Though we have superior speed, strength and skills, they still outnumber us. Plus, they've captured and used our own people to figure out how to weaken and eliminate us."

And Harlee had played an integral role in that process. Guilt washed over her. But why? She did the job she was trained to do, based on what her government told her about the lycans and vampires. She held onto her training like a lifeline, forcing the doubts away.

"Together, we are stronger than separate," Duncan said. "Lycans and vampires have forged an uneasy peace. We cannot fight the humans as well separately as we can united."

"Then why haven't the lycans and vampires allowed cross mating?" she wondered.

Adrian stood and leaned against one of the bookshelves. "Centuries ago, our people were lax about interaction between humans and their kind. The vampires and lycans created from blood interaction with humans developed a madness, the blood lust, which couldn't be contained. They became uncontrollable killers, preying on other humans. Of course this was attributed to the pure lycans and vampires, so we realized it would have to stop. But by then the blame had been cast in our direction. We became the enemy. We had to round up and kill the humans who had been turned and our people forbade blood contact with humans. That's where we still get the occasional rogues. Though we tried to get to all of them, we knew some had managed to slip through our nets. They're still out there."

Duncan nodded. "And vampires and lycans had always been at war for supremacy and control, but once the government began tracking us down and destroying us, we knew we had to join forces. Because of the nightmare the transfer of blood into humans had caused, our people theorized that cross breeding vampires and lycans would produce a similar result, or possibly one even worse. So it was outlawed."

"So no vampires and lycans had ever mated?" she asked.

"Not that we're aware of. If they had, we think we'd have known," Adrian said. "Until Stefan and Amelia, of course. And we still haven't determined the result of that union. You hold the key to those results, Harlee. So far, you seem okay."

Or so they thought. And if her luck held out, they'd keep on thinking that, because she couldn't give them the opportunity to discover who she was. Or rather, who she wasn't.

"We had just started working on what strategies to use to go about the experimental cross breeding," Adrian explained. "It's all tech/medical stuff so it's over our heads, but the bottom line is, the plans are on hold because of Stefan's death. Tensions are high and so is suspicion. But now that we have you, what we can learn from you might provide our tech people with information on how to go about it."

"Didn't Stefan and Amelia mate the...uh, natural way?" she asked.

"Yeah," Duncan said. "But we still don't know how it affects a child of that kind of union. Like Adrian said, you're the key."

"We've recently decided it's imperative for us to determine whether lycans and vampires can breed successfully. Increasing our numbers and possibly our powers can only help us if our fight with humans goes to all-out war. Their technology is growing, at least in some areas," Adrian said, disgust evident on his frowning face. "They have no idea how much we could benefit them. Instead, they concentrate on using our own people to develop weaponry to use against us."

"How can you benefit them?" Harlee asked, pushing aside that constant niggle of guilt at what they'd done to the vampires and lycans they'd captured.

"We've done a bit of our own testing here in the labs," Adrian explained. "Genetic testing, researching ways to assist humans in becoming more resistant to the diseases plaguing them. Our original goal was to come out of the darkness, to make peace with the humans by offering our assistance. We sent negotiators to discuss this. Only our negotiators didn't return."

"No, they were used," Duncan chimed in. "And now the negotiations have stopped but the humans are relentless in their quest to hunt us down and exterminate us. We have to hide who and what we are, maintain a cloak of secrecy that neither of our species want, because humans are too afraid of us to negotiate, to even let us demonstrate how we can help. Their paranoia is groundless, so we may yet have to go to war with them, if only to save ourselves."

The trickle of doubt within Harlee began to grow, and no matter how she tried to discount what Duncan and Adrian said to her, she could no longer ignore what they said. With the doubt, fear surfaced, and a sick feeling that they might just be right and humans had been wrong all along.

Dead wrong.

Duncan watched the mix of emotions cross Harlee's face. Confusion, fear, disbelief and finally resignation. He'd love to crawl into her mind and figure out what was going on in there. Trying to imagine what she was going through was impossible. He admired her strength in dealing with everything she'd learned in such a short period of time.

And her sass...he loved that about her. There was nothing more attractive than a woman who gave as good as she got, who showed no fear.

"What's up, everyone?"

He turned at the sound of a sexy voice, not at all surprised to find that voice attached to Annmarie. Speaking of sass, she was really something, all wrapped up in a petite, bombshell package that never failed to fire his imagination. His mind was always full of ideas of what they could do together. Too bad she was vampire and forbidden to him. Then again, when had "forbidden" ever stopped him?

"What are you doing here?" Adrian asked.

Annmarie arched a brow. "I came to see my new friend, if you don't mind," she said, ignoring her cousin's warning looks and taking a seat in the chair next to Harlee. "You look like you need to get out, get a little fresh air and party a bit."

"No," Adrian said curtly.

"I can speak for myself, thank you," Harlee said, lifting her chin. "Sounds like fun."

"Yes, it does," Annmarie replied before staring at Adrian. "And why not? Are you intending to keep her prisoner here until she agrees to fuck your brains out?"

Duncan chuckled at how easily Annmarie pushed Adrian's buttons. That kind of banter among kin made him miss his own family in Scotland, even though the work he did here was important. There was just something about the comfort of family, even if they did occasionally drive you crazy.

"What makes you think she's capable of fucking my brains out?" Adrian challenged, his gaze directed at Harlee, not his cousin.

The vampire was either completely daft or teasing. Duncan could smell Harlee's sexuality, banked like a smoldering fire and ready to ignite at the first touch of an accelerant. He was going to make damn sure he added fuel to her fire, though he wondered if she'd burn him alive.

"Keep it up, pal, and you may never find out," Harlee replied with a smirk of her own.

There it was. That spunk that made her so attractive. It wasn't hard to see the sparks flying between Adrian and Harlee. Some chemistry definitely at work there. He wondered if that had anything to do with her dominant side slowly coming to the surface. Was she inherently vampire instead of lycan? He supposed he'd have to wait patiently and see what developed, on both counts.

"So? Are we up for a little party? I was thinking *Blood and Guts*," Annmarie said.

Adrian rolled his eyes. "Yeah, throw her right into the fire on her first night."

"Not a bad idea, though," Duncan said, sending a pointed look to Adrian. "Might be a learning experience for her and step up the process a bit."

Raising both brows in thought, Adrian finally nodded. "You're right. *Blood and Guts* it is."

"Um, what's *Blood and Guts*?" Harlee asked, eyes wide. "Or do I even want to know?"

"Oh you'll love it," Annmarie replied with a grin. "I think we should go tonight."

"That sounds fun. I'd love to."

"Annmarie," Adrian warned.

"Oh quit being such a prude, Adrian," she replied. "Let the girl have a little bit of fun. She has to learn about us, right?"

He sighed. "I guess."

"Okay, then. Come on, honey. Let's spend the afternoon going over clothes. We'll have lunch, do our nails, hair and have a little girl fun before these men bore you to death in the library. I know exactly what you should wear. Ta ta, gentlemen," she said with a wave, dragging Harlee out the door by her arm.

"I had some paperwork to do anyway," Duncan said, suppressing a chuckle at Adrian's disgruntled look.

Adrian shook his head and muttered a curse as he stepped out of the library. Duncan followed, grinning at this turn of events. He had very few friends among the vampires and he counted Adrian as one of those few. But his friend had control issues. And Duncan had a feeling that between Annmarie and Harlee, he'd have very little.

It should prove to be an interesting night.

* * * * *

The driving beat of the bass could be heard from the parking lot of the two-story club, a converted warehouse painted all black, even the windows. Only a red neon sign pointed out its entrance. Annmarie sauntered past the long line and up to the front door, dragging one fingernail over the cheek of the huge bouncer outside, who waved them in.

"Know people in all the right places?" Harlee asked.

Annmarie grinned. "Or all the wrong places."

Harlee felt underdressed, the cool night air blowing underneath the tiny black stretchy miniskirt Annmarie had insisted she wear. And the little scrap of material covering only her pussy lips could in no way constitute underwear. She'd been scandalized when Annmarie took her shopping in the Dark Moon shopping complex that afternoon and picked out clothing and underthings that Harlee wouldn't have purchased in a million years. But then again, Harlee hadn't been the one doing the buying since she had no money, so she couldn't be choosy. The belly-skimming silk halter top in blood red admittedly felt sexy and sensuous against her nipples, the breeze ruffling the material against the puckered buds, making them stand up noticeably.

Or at least Adrian and Duncan noticed. Flanked on either side of her as they escorted her through the throng of people waiting in line at the *Blood and Guts*, casting their gazes throughout the crowd as if an assassin lurked within the group.

Honestly, it wasn't as if anyone knew who the hell she was. Even they didn't know, so she had no idea what they were worried about. Though there was the matter of Stefan's murder and the fact she was his daughter did put her in jeopardy.

Correction. *They* thought she was his daughter. But if they thought so, other vampires and lycans thought so too. In fact, Adrian had grumbled about it the entire way to the club, complaining they couldn't protect her in a crowd like this. Annmarie brushed him off and told him Harlee had to learn about their ways and what better way to do that than to see them in action.

Whatever "action" meant. She'd been too afraid to ask.

Annmarie grabbed Harlee's hand and dragged her forward, away from the heat of Adrian and Duncan's sides. Harlee craned her neck to see them following, Duncan with an amused grin and Adrian with an annoyed glare. She couldn't resist smiling at Adrian's irritation.

The club was dark and it took awhile for her eyes to acclimate. The place was completely packed with wall-to-wall bodies. People constantly brushed against her as Annmarie dragged her around until she finally decided on a table between the long bar and the huge dance floor. Silvery lights overhead shimmered onto the mirror-like floor, reflecting like shots of lightning from floor to ceiling. The throng of bodies gyrating to the heavy beat of the music seemed to sparkle like a comet, all melded together into one streak of silvery glitter.

A waitress came over and Annmarie held up four fingers, then hollered, "Blood and Guts!" The waitress nodded and slipped away. Harlee hoped the drink was a euphemism for something else.

Once her eyes adjusted, she stared at the jaw-dropping scene on the dance floor. People weren't just dancing, they were practically having sex! She'd never considered herself a prude, but holy hell, the amount of flesh revealed and the movements as couples clung to each other in passionate embraces had her face heating. Her gaze shot to her companions. Annmarie was rocking to the music, Duncan's gaze was fixated on the action of the dancers, his nostrils flaring and his eyes darkening. Adrian was looking at her, his half-hooded eyes sexier than anything she'd witnessed on the dance floor.

Her visual acuity improved dramatically, which surprised her considering the dimly lit club. His eyes heated, swirls of amber weaving and glowing within the chocolate orbs. She felt the touch of his eyes as they roamed from her face to her neck, lingering at her throat. She felt her blood heat.

She hadn't seem him change in any way, but she could well imagine his fangs sliding down, sharp points glittering like diamonds in the night, piercing the tender flesh of her neck. His lips would cover her skin, suckling the blood from her artery. She'd feel it pulsing throughout her body, rushing to give him the sustenance he craved. And in return, her body would begin pulsing too, only not in her neck. Her pussy vibrated, thrumming like a heartbeat deep in her womb, moistening and opening for an invasion she craved so deeply it hurt.

When the waitress returned with their drinks, she blinked, profoundly shocked by her wayward thoughts. She felt as thought she had just awakened from a deep sleep, haunting, sexual dreams clinging to her reality.

Whoa. That was beyond strange. Had he mesmerized her in some way? With his head now turned, she couldn't see his face to gauge his reaction. Had he felt what she felt? Had he caused it or was it something else?

"Drink this," Annmarie said, sliding a glass of red liquid in front of her. Harlee cast a dubious glance at Annmarie, who laughed and said, "It's not blood, silly. Trust me."

She took a sip, surprised at the sweet flavor. "Oh, this is good!"

"Told you. It'll relax you a bit. You're so wound up I can feel the tension across the table. You need to let go a little, honey."

Let go? If she let go any more she'd probably straddle one of these men and fuck him right here in the club. She doubted anyone would even notice considering the activities going on around her. Everywhere she looked couples grappled in passion. Oh, they were still clothed...mostly. Then again you could do a lot while still clothed, and she'd already glimpsed more than one man's hand disappear down a woman's blouse or into her pants, had seen the women's eyes roll back in ecstasy as the men touched them intimately.

Eroticism and sensual play was the game here. And no one blinked or looked at these people like they were doing anything out of the ordinary.

"Vampires and lycans have a natural inclination toward sexual play, both intimately and in a group setting. We don't attempt to hide our needs or desires. When we want someone, we're open about it, taking what is offered. Both our men and women are very satisfied," Adrian said.

Whispered, actually, his warm, spicy breath sailing across her cheek. When he brushed her hair away from her neck, she shivered and tensed. Her nipples hardened and she was grateful for the darkness. Though when she moved away to look at his face, he was staring at her breasts.

"You think I can't see in the dark?"

She shivered again, this time from a primal heat that coiled deep in her belly and flamed outward, rocketing her senses into awareness of the man sitting beside her.

"I'm going to dance. Want to join me?"

Harlee nodded at Annmarie, desperately needing distance from Adrian. Whenever he was around she lost all her senses, tuning in to him, his voice, the way he smelled.

It was time to focus elsewhere, to use the dance floor as an opportunity to survey her surroundings, memorize faces in case she needed to point them out later and look for a way to escape.

The music had a driving beat, evoking thoughts of wild sexual abandon. She laughed when Annmarie grabbed her hands and began to wiggle her hips in time to the music. Harlee followed suit, losing herself in the music, feeling the bass reverberate against her, entering her body and loosening her inhibitions.

She'd always loved dancing and had somehow always managed to choose dates who didn't. Invariably she and a few of her girlfriends would end up on the dance floor together, ignoring the men and enjoying themselves.

That's what she did now, moving in time to the rhythm of the song, closing her eyes and letting the music catapult her into another time, another place, where she was free to do whatever she wanted, had no responsibilities, no worries. The crowd closed around her, bodies bumping against her from all sides. She and Annmarie drew closer, laughing and sweating as the tempo increased and they moved faster. When it was over, she was drained, thirsty and exhilarated.

"I need a drink," she yelled at Annmarie as another song began.

"I'm going to hang here and dance for awhile," Annmarie replied.

Harlee nodded and walked back to the table, conscious of two pairs of eyes watching her.

Two faces with intense expressions as hot as a roaring winter fire stared at her, lust and need nearly palpable. If she thought she was going to cool off at the table, she was wrong.

She had a feeling things were just beginning to heat up.

Chapter Five

ဢ

Duncan wasn't sure which woman to ogle. Hell, that had always been his problem, and why he hadn't yet mated. Too many choices and they all looked good. And watching Harlee and Annmarie dance together sent his cock into a roaring erection.

Harlee walked toward them, her face flushed and a fine sheen of perspiration glistening on her skin. He wanted to lick those droplets off every inch of her, then slide his tongue into her pussy and eat her until she screamed and shifted into the lycan he knew her to be.

No creature as filled with sensuality as Harlee could be anything but lycan. Then again, Annmarie was a unique animal in her own right. Though vampire, and he typically had no desires for vamps, she was a hot one. A wild thing needing the right man to tame her. If only he were allowed to do so. He'd love to get her in a room, chain her up and give her the beast he knew she needed. Fucking her would be a once in a lifetime experience.

Harlee sat down, her breasts rising and falling against the thin silk top.

Adrian signaled for the waitress to bring another round of drinks.

"Had fun, did you?" Adrian asked.

She smiled. God she was breathtaking when she smiled. It lit up her entire face and made her eyes sparkle like emeralds. "I haven't danced in ages and your cousin is a dynamo. It's hard to keep up with her."

Duncan had a feeling most people would find it difficult to keep up with Annmarie. He could, though. And then some. "You held your own just fine, lass."

"Oh I don't know about that. Just look at her. She's so free-spirited."

He turned around and searched the dance floor, finding Annmarie just at the edge of the throng of bodies gyrating to a jungle-like beat. She'd found two vamps to tangle with. One in front of her, one behind her, sandwiching her between them as she rubbed her breasts against one and her ass against the other. Her micro-miniskirt and barely-there top made her look wanton and untamed.

The men dancing with her knew it too. One skimmed the sides of her breasts, the one behind her lifted her skirt and squeezed her ass, then pressed his jean-clad erection against her. Annmarie's head fell back on the man's shoulder, her mouth opening and her tongue snaking over her bottom lip.

Duncan had never seen anything hotter. Or anything that pissed him off more. Hell, pretty soon they'd be fucking her right on the dance floor!

"Sonofabitch!" he muttered. "The bastards have their hands all over her!"

"So they do," Adrian said. "Typical."

Duncan craned his head around, irritated at Adrian's amused look. "She's your cousin. Aren't you going to do something about it?"

Adrian shrugged. "Like what? She's a grown woman. She does what she wants. And she can take care of herself. And it's not like anyone can say anything to stop her."

"Wanna bet?" Duncan was furious. He didn't know why, but boiling rage churned inside him and he wanted to tear those two male vamps to shreds.

"Give it your best shot," Adrian said.

Duncan rose and headed toward the throng of sweaty bodies undulating to the music. Stopping in front of Annmarie, he leveled a glare at the two vamps sandwiching her. They bared their fangs but wisely said nothing.

"Something you want, lycan?" Annmarie asked, flashing a dazzling smile.

"Yeah. I want you to stop dancing with these assholes." Part of him couldn't believe he'd said it. What the hell was wrong with him? Sex was a regular thing at *Blood and Guts*. Hell, he'd seen a lot more here than the little bout of foreplay Annmarie engaged in. Yet it still bugged him. And if there was one thing Duncan always listened to, it was his gut instinct. It had never been wrong before.

Annmarie turned to face him, hands on her hips, her full breasts thrusting out toward him as she caught her breath. "Why? You want to manhandle me instead?"

"Doubt you could handle it, lass," he quipped. If she thought to challenge him into backing down, she'd chosen the wrong man.

"Lycans are forbidden to mix with vampires," one of the vamps said.

Duncan leveled a growl in his direction. "And lycans are forbidden to kill vampires too. But I doubt there's anyone here capable of stopping me from tearing you two to shreds. So get the fuck out of here before I decide to eat your scrawny asses."

"Yeah. He'd rather eat *me* instead," Annmarie said with a cocky grin then turned to her two dance partners. "Thanks for the dance, guys. I think I've been challenged, so I'll catch up with you later."

The two vamps grumbled, but obviously when Annmarie dismissed someone, they knew better than to argue. Glaring at Duncan, they moved away in search of easier pickings.

She arched a brow expectantly. "Okay, lycan. Now that you've got me, what do you intend to do with me?"

He had several ideas, none of them legal. But just then a slower song started, and he grabbed Annmarie, dragging her into his arms. "Let's dance."

A tiny smile danced along the corner of her lips as she reached up and wound her arms around his neck. "That'll do. For a start."

Harlee watched in fascination at the way Annmarie held court with three men vying for her attention. Amazing. She had them all wrapped around her finger like puppets on a string.

Even Duncan, who managed to get rid of his two rivals. Clearly he felt something for Annmarie, lust if nothing else. Should she be annoyed that Annmarie was flirting with Duncan or that he was interested in her? As she watched the way he looked at Annmarie, she realized she felt no jealousy whatsoever. Then again, why should she? She had no feelings for either Duncan or Adrian. She was supposed to fuck both of them, not marry them.

And she intended to do neither, no matter what her body wanted.

"Come on," Adrian said, startling her. He held out his hand for her.

"Where to?"

"Let's move where we can see the two of them better. This should be fun to watch."

She grinned, surprised he'd be the least bit interested in watching the interplay between Duncan and Annmarie. But she slipped her hand in his and allowed him to pull her toward the edge of the platform overlooking the dance floor. He moved her so that her back rested against his chest, a position that made giant butterflies flap their wings in her stomach. How was she supposed to watch the scene in front of her when the man behind her captured all her attention?

His scent was spicy, like something from the forest. Earthy, primal and arousing her own primitive instincts to take this man and make him her own.

She shook her head and tried to take a step forward, but his arm snaked around her middle and pulled her back against him.

"You aren't going anywhere. Stay put and watch."

How dare he tell her what to do? Stomping on his foot was her first thought, followed by a sharp jab in the ribs with her elbow, but she ended up doing neither. Not when it felt so damn good to be held by him. His body was warm...hot, actually, not at all like she'd expect a vampire's to be. Then again, she was growing suspicious that she had this whole vampire/lycan thing wrong. Or at least the government did. They just weren't the way the government portrayed them. And as for how she felt about Adrian, she simply wouldn't analyze her strange physical reactions. Instead, she focused on Annmarie and Duncan dirty dancing.

Though dirty wasn't really the right word to describe what they were doing on the dance floor. Erotic, eye-popping, lust-filled gyrating was how Harlee would describe it.

Duncan lifted one of Annmarie's legs and held it as he pulled her closer, rocking his pelvis between her thighs. Annmarie hooked her leg around the back of Duncan's thigh and rubbed her breasts against his chest.

The look he gave her took Harlee's breath away. Primal, needy...hungry. He practically sneered at Annmarie, but Harlee didn't read it as anger. It was purely and simply lust. And Annmarie had a dreamy expression on her face as she gazed intently at Duncan, desire clear in her eyes.

They weren't talking, but they were communicating with their bodies as they undulated together. When Duncan lifted Annmarie so a leg hung on either side of his upper thigh, Harlee gasped and then held her breath, imagining the feel of Annmarie's clit in contact with the hard muscle of Duncan's thigh. Sparks shot between her legs as she visualized the touch of aroused skin against denim. Annmarie's tiny little skirt rode up, exposing her hips. She wore no underwear.

Harlee really should be shocked at their behavior, but for the life of her all she could feel was an incessant, pounding ache between her legs. Her clit was a knot of needy nerve endings desperate for a touch, a lick, the flick of a finger — anything to release the pressure steadily building inside her. Had they drugged her, maybe something in the drinks? These feelings were so bizarre, so unlike her. Wild, primitive, making her think about doing things she'd never wanted to do before.

"Makes you hot watching them, doesn't it?" Adrian asked, palming her hip and drawing her closer.

His erection pulsed with a life force that called to her, demanding she take notice. Not that she could have missed it. Part of her wanted to slide her hand behind her and palm his hard-on, test its length, its thickness, and caress it until he bent her over the railing in front of her and pounded his cock into her aching, needy pussy.

Annmarie and Duncan weren't helping one bit either. Annmarie rode Duncan's thigh as if she were impaled on his cock. Her nails dug into the bare flesh of his upper arms, her head tilted back as she gyrated against him. Duncan held her on his leg with one huge hand, squeezing her buttocks and letting her seek her pleasure. His jaw clenched tight, sweat dripping from his brow. His hard-on was huge and straining against his jeans. Harlee half expected him to unzip his pants and plunge it into Annmarie right there on the dance floor.

Oh, hell, she hoped he would. She was dying to see it, needed to see it in a way she couldn't explain.

"Answer me, Harlee."

She didn't want to. Or at least one half of her didn't want to. The part of her that feared these unfamiliar sensations, this need to break free and go completely wild like Annmarie. It *had* to be drugs. She'd never felt like this before. This wasn't her normal behavior at all.

Adrian rocked against her, pressing his cock against her ass. Heat seared her pussy. It wept its need for him, for his shaft. She bit down on her lip to keep from begging him to fuck her.

"You can't hide from me," he whispered, his breath sailing across her cheek. "I can smell you. You're hot, aroused and desperate to come. I'll bet if you were alone you'd run to the ladies room and fuck yourself, wouldn't you, baby?"

Oh, God, how could he know how she felt? How could he have tapped into the need that poured from her when she'd tried her best to remain immune and completely still?

"A vampire's senses are acute, Harlee. When you learn to bring out your own, you'll know. We see more, feel more, can sense emotions and smell blood, fear, excitement and lust on another. Right now I can tell you how many times your heart beats in a minute. It's faster than normal because you're turned on watching Annmarie ride Duncan's thigh. The tangy scent of your blood calls to me as one vampire calls to another. It's inexplicable, yet as elemental to us as breathing is to humans."

He slid one hand down her arm and over her hip, letting it rest there, kneading her flesh as he pumped his denim-clad shaft against her backside. Her legs trembled and she fought to still her rasping breaths.

"I can smell your pussy," he continued, "that sweet, musky scent of aroused female that makes me want to draw your hair aside and sink my teeth into your neck." He moved her hair away, his hot breath teasing the small curls at her nape. She could almost feel the soft touch of his tongue against her skin and shuddered, fighting the urge to beg him to press his lips against her throat, to bite her.

"Do you like to be bitten, Harlee? Maybe no one's ever bitten you, but I'll bet you wanted them to. And not just on your neck either. I'll bet you'd like me to take a little taste of your inner thigh, wouldn't you? Or even better, scrape my teeth against your clit until you scream and flood my face with your cum."

A moan escaped her lips. She couldn't stand this. It wasn't fair. Unaccustomed to being seduced, she could only hang there helpless, suspended on a rack of aching desperation, with Adrian her only rescue. She needed him. She didn't want to, but dammit she needed him.

"Now, admit that watching Annmarie fuck herself against Duncan's thigh turns you on. Tell me you want the same thing, that sweet release that only I can give you right now."

She'd always prided herself on her grit, her inner strength, but right now every ounce of self-control she'd ever possessed had fled, leaving in its wake raw need and an arousal so potent it brought her to tears. "Yes, goddamit! I want it, Adrian!"

Adrian groaned in triumph, his cock so hard it could easily burst free of his pants. Christ, he'd never wanted a woman as much as he wanted Harlee. And her resistance to what she obviously wanted only increased his lust. Because he knew she fought demons inside herself, knew she wasn't holding back because she didn't need him, but because she did need him. And it scared her.

Hell, it scared him too, but he was powerless to resist her. He was as much under her spell as she was under his, and he'd waited long enough already. Moving his hand under her skirt, he caressed the smooth flesh of her buttocks, inhaling her scent, letting it fill him and boil his blood. The tiny thong she wore was the only barrier between his questing fingers and her pussy. He slipped his hand between the flimsy material and her skin and yanked hard, the panties giving way easily. Free of that encumbrance, he searched between her taut buttocks, smiling when she tensed as his fingers brushed against her anus.

"You'd like me to take you there, wouldn't you?" he whispered, his tongue flicking out to capture her earlobe while he teased the tiny puckered hole of her ass. Instead of flinching, she moved against his fingers, her shuddering breath signaling her assent. God, she tasted sweet, her skin a sugared honey that just made him hungry to lick her everywhere else. He moved his hand further in and felt the moist cream of her arousal dripping from her slit. Shuddering, he pressed his throbbing cock against her hip. The need to be inside her drove him, his cock pulsing as he imagined how hot and tight she'd be.

Regaining control of his senses, he also knew she wasn't ready to be taken just yet, and for some reason it was important that she was. He was satisfied enough right now, just touching her, smelling her and feeling her body tremble against his.

When he slid one finger between the swollen folds of her cunt, she gasped, her body going rigid before shuddering and spilling liquid desire all over his hand. Her pussy pulsed and latched onto his finger like a life preserver, squeezing as he worked it all the way in.

"You are so fucking hot," he whispered, pumping his finger in and out in time to the driving beat of the music. "Will your pussy grab my dick the same way, Harlee?" He could already imagine her tissues surrounding him, taking all of him in and then tightening around his shaft. His balls ached for release, but he was more interested in her release.

"Watch them," he said, slipping another finger into her pussy. "Watch Duncan and Annmarie and imagine he's doing that to you."

Duncan had turned Annmarie toward them. She gripped the railing of the dance floor as he positioned himself behind her, his hand lifting the front of her skirt so he could pet her bare pussy.

Harlee saw the silver ring dangling from the hood of Annmarie's clit, imagining the exquisite pleasure a woman could feel when that tiny little loop was played with. Duncan did just that, covering her sex with his large hand and moving it back and forth over Annmarie's pussy, flicking the ring with his finger and circling her clit with deliberate caresses.

She'd never watched another couple have sex before. Her breath caught and held as sensations bombarded her. The visuals of Duncan's fingers sliding into Annmarie's pussy, the look on her face when he buried his long, thick fingers deep inside her then used his other hand to play with her clit. Adrian's movements mirrored Duncan's as if he too watched them play and wanted to give Harlee the same pleasure.

Her pussy quaked and squeezed, tightening around Adrian's hot fingers. Cream spilled from her and trickled down her thighs, further evidence of her fierce arousal. She felt wanton, wicked and thoroughly exposed, yet the thought that others might be watching her in the same way she watched Duncan and Annmarie didn't bother her as much as she had imagined it would. She looked around, noticing only the frantic gyrations and groping of the other couples who paid no attention to what Adrian was doing to her.

Yet it still excited her to know that he touched her here, in public, where anyone could watch the action. Past the point of reason, she didn't care if anyone looked, if an entire crowd gathered to cheer her. Her only focus right now was on the incredible sensations Adrian evoked as he pulled his fingers from her pussy and swirled her lubrication over her swollen clit.

Shards of intense pleasure shot straight to her core, her bud a tight knot of sensitized nerve endings just waiting to explode. Duncan leaned Annmarie back against his chest, her legs spread wide as he fucked her pussy relentlessly with his fingers. Annmarie watched her, smiling as if she understood Harlee's pleasure, seemingly oblivious to the fact that her skirt was hiked up over her hips, her pussy exposed for everyone to see. Duncan's face was filled with tight determination as he played Annmarie's clit like a musician who intimately knew exactly what to do to make his instrument sing. His gaze was trained on Harlee too and a sexy smile lit up his turquoise eyes. It was the most erotic thing Harlee had ever seen or done and added fuel to the flame ready to explode inside her.

"Your pussy's tightening around my fingers, Harlee," Adrian said, his voice tight and husky. "Damn, I want my cock inside you when you come. And I will…soon. You can bet on it. Now come for me, baby. I want to feel your cream pouring over my hand."

At that moment Annmarie thrust her pussy against Duncan's hand. Her head tilted back and sharp canines slid down over her eyeteeth. She growled, snarled, the look on her face a mix of ecstasy and feral heat. She was coming.

Harlee was damn close to doing the same thing. Adrian plunged his fingers deep, using his other hand to tug at her clit.

An orgasm rocketed through her entire body, making her shudder and cry out as a flood of cream poured from her. Her pussy squeezed Adrian's fingers as waves of pleasure crashed over her. She held onto his arms like a lifeline, digging her nails into his skin. Her climax was relentless, cataclysmic in intensity. She rode it out, gnashing her teeth and crying out until her lungs hurt.

Adrian held her until she found her balance again, then smoothed her skirt down. Duncan and Annmarie stepped off the dance floor. He didn't even hold her hand and she didn't seem to mind. Harlee supposed for them, it had been nothing more than just a little foreplay. From what she gathered, sex was as natural to vampires and lycans as breathing.

"After that wild ride, I need a double," Annmarie said with a wink as she stopped in front of them. "Looks like you had a pretty good time too," she added. "I'll order you another drink."

Duncan followed, stepping up to her and reaching for her hand, pressing a kiss to her palm. "Thanks for the visual," he said, then headed back to their table.

Despite the crashing orgasm that curled her toes, Harlee admitted a tiny sense of disappointment in the whole thing. Didn't anyone feel anything besides the physical rush of pleasure? Was sex really as unimportant and matter-of-fact as she thought? Maybe she put too much emphasis on it. It wasn't like Adrian or Duncan had any feelings for her, or she for them. So what was the big deal?

He hadn't even kissed her. That was the big deal. There had been touching. Hot, mind-numbing touching. But she hadn't tasted him. Okay, so it was important to her. So she was a romantic at heart. So what? She'd never let on that the episode had been anything more than a physical release. And she'd sure as hell needed that.

She turned to head to the table, but Adrian's hand around her upper arm stopped her. She looked up at him, shocked at the look of primal, unhidden lust in his eyes. A quick glance at his crotch told her he was still as hard as stone. She might have gotten release, but he didn't. Would he ask her to get him off now? Right there in front of everyone? If sex meant so little to them, she had no doubt that's why he stopped her.

"Touch me," he demanded, reaching for her hand and placing it on the huge bulge straining against his jeans.

Harlee felt the throbbing beat of his pulse, unable to resist pressing her palm over his erection. Adrian sucked in a breath, then grabbed her wrist and pulled her hand away, using his hold on her to jerk her against his chest. His lips covered hers, taking in her shocked gasp. His tongue invaded her mouth, not hard and insistent like she expected, but soft and exploratory, gently stroking her tongue and sliding his lips against hers in a gentle, sensual way that rocked her libido all over again. She whimpered at the tenderness of his mouth against hers, wishing she could spend hours just kissing him, but he pulled away, his glassy eyes meeting hers, tension evident in the hard muscles straining under her hands.

"I'm so goddamned hard I could explode right now," he said. "But I'm saving that for when I'm inside you. When I can undress you slowly, kiss every inch of your body starting with that sexy mouth of yours. Then I'll bury my cock in you and really make you scream, because what happened just now wasn't nearly enough, Harlee. Get ready for it, because it's going to happen."

He walked away, leaving her standing there, her jaw dropping at his words. Shock left her unable to move. Her mind couldn't process all that had happened. Though a small part of her screamed for logic, to realize she was now alone, that she should make a run for it, her body betrayed her, compelling her to move back to the table and sit down with them.

No. She had to fight against the urge to go to them. This might be her one and only chance to break free, to run like hell back to safety, and shake off whatever magical spell they'd placed on her.

Scanning the room, she took a few steps back, then entered the throng of dancers. They'd simply think she was looking for a bathroom, even started to head in that direction just in case they were watching her.

She found the restrooms, all right, but there was no exit door anywhere. Hurriedly searching the rest of the club, she soon realized that the only door was the front door, and she couldn't get to it without passing Adrian, Duncan and Annmarie.

Shit! She had to think, find a way out.

"Are you okay?"

The touch of a hand on her shoulder had her gasping in shock. She whipped around to find Annmarie standing there.

"I'm fine. Just…looking for the restroom."

Annmarie grinned. "It is kind of crowded in here and hard to find anything if you're unfamiliar. Come on, I'll show you."

Having no choice but to follow, she went with Annmarie, knowing her one and only chance of escape was gone. And she still felt woozy, like she'd had too much to drink. Her mind and body felt strangely hot. Her thoughts were full of sex, the need to return to Adrian and Duncan nearly overwhelming and driving her into a fully aroused state once again.

What the hell was happening to her?

Chapter Six

❧

Harlee sat quietly at the breakfast table, afraid to even look up from her plate. If she did, she knew she'd turn a bright crimson having to face Duncan, Adrian and Annmarie.

She'd lain awake nearly the entire night, tossing and turning and unable to sleep despite the blistering orgasm Adrian had given her. That was one of the reasons she couldn't sleep! How could she have allowed herself to let go like that? It had to be some kind of mind trick, a drug or something that made her act the way she had, because it certainly wasn't her typical behavior to allow a guy to slip his fingers inside her pussy and take her over the edge in the middle of a dance club. Her own body betrayed her, and these mixed-up desires and emotions she felt weren't her own feelings, but something they'd implanted in her.

What else could possibly explain her complete turnaround in personality?

"You're quiet this morning, Harl. Is something wrong?"

She did a quick lookup from her plate, smiled at Annmarie and said, "No, I'm fine. Just concentrating on my food." Then she looked down again.

"You haven't touched it," Adrian said.

She refused to look at him. Already the heat singed her cheeks and neck, embarrassment flooding her skin with a rush of warmth. "I'm not hungry."

"Lass, look up," Duncan coaxed, his voice soothing and gentle.

With a deep sigh, she lifted her head to find three pairs of eyes focused on her. This was worse than she could have imagined. What must they think of her?

"What's wrong?" Duncan asked.

"Nothing's wrong. I just didn't sleep well last night."

"Well, hell, woman. I made you come so hard you were screaming. If that didn't relax you enough to sleep, I don't know what would."

Oh God, did they always talk so matter-of-factly about sex?

"I slept like the dead last night," Annmarie quipped, shooting a wink at Duncan. Duncan replied with a nod and a half smile that kicked the heat in the room up another ten degrees.

She was going to simply sit there and self-combust.

"Are you embarrassed about what happened last night?" Adrian asked.

"No!" she shouted, then winced as she realized the denial only confirmed his statement.

"Honey, we told you that we're pretty frisky and out there with sex," Annmarie explained. "It's really no big deal."

"It is to me. Sex means something to me. I don't take it lightly and I don't...do what I did last night."

"You're changing," Adrian said. "The vampire blood within you is calling to your sex drive."

"And the lycan blood within her," Duncan countered.

"True," Annmarie added. "The combination is pretty heady. Add the two together and it's no wonder it hit you so hard and so fast."

Or maybe they were controlling her and making her act this way. Just being in the same room with Duncan and Adrian this morning made her body fire up hot and ready.

Her panties were wet and it was only eight-thirty in the morning. She was hot, aroused and primed for sex. Over breakfast. Geez, there was definitely something wrong with her. She had to get away from these two men, away from this environment that created havoc inside her mind.

"You'll get used to it, honey," Annmarie assured her, flipping her long hair behind her with the sweep of her hand. "After awhile you won't think twice about having sex or watching it. Sometimes things get crazy here and you could see sex on the stairwells or in the kitchen. When we want it, we go after it no matter where it is."

"Speak for yourself, cousin," Adrian said, glaring at her. "Not all of us fuck like rabbits in public. Some of us are more discreet."

Annmarie snorted.

"Oh I beg to differ, Adrian. I think I know as well as anyone that your statement isn't true."

Harlee's gaze shot to the doorway. Sara entered, her eyes focused only on Adrian. Dressed elegantly in cream slacks and a sapphire blue blouse that highlighted her ample breasts, her golden hair piled high on top of her head, she looked like a regal princess. As she passed behind his chair, she lightly trailed her fingers over his shoulders before slipping into the seat next to his.

Okay, so Adrian had a past with Sara. Or maybe he had a present with Sara. Why did that thought make her heart hurt? So vampires were sluts. Harlee certainly didn't have a claim on Adrian, despite what happened between them last night.

"Drop it, Sara," Adrian warned, picking up his fork and resuming his meal.

"Just trying to make sure Harlee gets accurate information. Just because your cousin is a whore doesn't mean Harlee needs to think she's going to end up the same way." Sara turned to her and offered a kind, warm smile. "We're not all as nonconforming as Annmarie, darling. While it's true there are certain times the bloodlust gets the best of us and we have to have sex while the moment is hot, most of the time we're quite discreet."

"Blow it out your ass, bitch," Annmarie stated as matter-of-factly as if she'd just bid Sara a good morning. "You and Adrian, up against the wall at the top of the stairs? Please. Spare me your holier-than-thou sermon and just admit you like a good fuck as well as I do."

Sara's eyes widened then narrowed as she shot Annmarie a vicious glare. But then the lines on her forehead relaxed and she shrugged. "I don't know why I bother trying to have a civil conversation with someone like you."

"I don't know why you bother trying to have *any* kind of conversation with me," Annmarie quipped.

"Knock it off, both of you," Adrian said, then looked past Sara toward Harlee. "Look. We all like to fuck. It's inherent. You'll want it more often and you'll want it harder, like an animal. You'll get used to it soon enough. It's part of your nature."

Not part of *her* nature. She was human, but they didn't know it. They just assumed she was in the throes of some beastly transformation, and she had to make sure they continued to think that way. Which meant she had to start acting like she really was transforming.

"Well, it's all damned uncomfortable and I'm just not used to it. Sorry."

Sara patted her hand. "It's okay, honey. I can't even imagine how difficult this must be for you. First the big revelation that you're not who and what you thought you were, and then all the physiological changes going on inside you. It's no wonder you're a little stressed. We all understand."

She offered Sara a weak smile. "Thanks. I appreciate that."

Duncan's phone rang, and thankfully she stopped being the center of everyone's attention as he began to argue with someone on the other end of the line. After a few curt responses, he flipped the phone off and looked to Adrian. "Lester wants to meet Harlee."

"Then tell him to get over here," Adrian said.

"Can't. You know since Stefan's death he's been in seclusion. Until we figure out who killed Stefan, Lester could possibly be the next target for assassination. I've got security tight around him and I want him to stay put."

"Who's Lester?" Harlee asked.

"Stefan's younger brother. Your uncle," Duncan replied. "He wants us to bring you to the family home this afternoon. It's about time you were introduced to the lycan side of your family."

Her uncle. Or rather, they thought he was her uncle. "And he wants to meet me?"

"Of course, darlin'," Duncan said with a smile. "It's important you meet both sides of your family."

An idea she didn't relish. Being here was bad enough. Then again, it meant travel, and travel meant the possibility of escape. "When do we go?"

"We'll check with Robert and get his okay for you to travel to the lycan mansion. Once that's done, we'll go as soon as you're ready," Duncan said.

She was ready in less than an hour. Showered, her hair dried and makeup applied. Of course she had to choose another one of the so-not-her-style outfits that Annmarie had given her, this time a short red stretchy skirt and black halter. Way too revealing to meet anyone, much less a relative. Then again, these vampires and lycans did things differently.

As she, Duncan and Adrian drove to Lester's home, Harlee actually started to feel nervous, as if she were about to meet someone she really was related to. Bizarre how her feelings had become all jumbled these past couple days.

She supposed that blindfolding her was out of the question now that she knew who and what she allegedly was. They drove outside the city, climbing uphill toward the mountains. Her breath caught when they pulled into a gated community, Duncan nodding at the fierce-looking guard who controlled the tall gates. The house was tall and imposing, a dark brown stone and brick mansion with towers at either end and no doubt enough room for an entire city of people to live in.

"I hope he's not the only one who lives here," Harlee said.

"Hardly," Duncan replied. "This is where most of the lycans live who are part of the clan in this area."

"How many is that?"

"Roughly a hundred."

Now it was clear why they needed such a huge place. "How do you keep the government from finding you?"

Duncan grinned and stopped the car in front of the mansion. "Rich people have big houses. The Leveaux holdings are sizeable."

"Leveaux?" she asked.

"Family name. Your family name, lass."

"As is the Baine family name," Adrian added.

Now it made sense. Funny how she'd never thought to ask about the surnames. "So Adrian is a Baine?"

He nodded.

"And Duncan is a…"

"Pain in the ass," Adrian teased.

"Funny," Duncan replied. "No, my family lives in Scotland. My last name is Kennard."

"What are you doing over here?" she asked.

"Been over here for quite some time, lass," he said. "So long about all I have left of my roots is a little of my brogue. Though occasionally a few Gaelic words slip out."

"So what would make more of them slip out?" she teased, wondering if she'd be able to hear him speak Gaelic to her. Such a romantic language.

"Sex," he replied.

Adrian coughed. Duncan laughed. Harlee shook her head.

"Okay. I'd probably pick more up if surrounded by my kinfolk. I always do when I visit home."

"Do you miss your family?"

"Sometimes. But you'll find among the lycans, and the vampires too, that we're all kin of some form or another."

So if she really was a part of both clans, she would be a mix of Leveaux and Baine. Interesting. "So you all didn't originate here?"

"Most of us are nomads," Duncan said, slipping the keys from the ignition and exiting the car. As they walked up the front stairs onto the enormous porch, he added, "Both lycans and vampires have moved out of necessity."

"True," Adrian said. "Between our bloody history and the human governments determined to exterminate us, we've constantly had to put down new roots. That means we're all over the world now."

She had so many questions, so much information and history she wanted to ask about both clans, but at that moment the front door opened and another stern, gigantic bodyguard blocked the doorway. He nodded when he saw Duncan and stepped away from the door.

Very similar to the Dark Moon holdings, the lycan home was enormous. Old world and gothic with incredibly expensive artwork decorating the walls and ancient tapestries hung throughout the downstairs. Duncan took her on a quick tour and Harlee was confused, passing by more hallways and staircases than she could ever remember. If she had to wander around this place alone, she'd be lost for sure.

They stopped in one room that had two sofas next to a fireplace. Very cozy and intimate, a few end tables and comfortable chairs were scattered about. She could see herself tucked in here on a snowy night, curled up next to a roaring fire while she read a book and drank a cup of tea.

Whoa. Where had that come from? She wasn't staying here, this wasn't her home and despite its warmth and comfort, she was so far out of her element it wasn't even funny. Instead of admiring the décor, she should be looking for a way out. What kind of an agent was she?

Not a very good one, apparently.

A tall, thin woman brought in a tray filled with coffee and tea, setting it onto the coffee table in front of them, then slipped out without a word. Soon after two of the big burly types walked in, followed by an older gentleman. Broad and muscular, with a full head of white hair and a very wide smile, he hurried over to Harlee and grasped both her hands in his.

"My niece, daughter of my brother, welcome to the Leveaux clan. I am Lester, brother of Stefan." Then he leaned in and kissed both her cheeks.

Harlee liked him immediately. There was a warmth to him that made her feel instantly comfortable. "It's nice to meet you, Lester."

"Sit down. I want to know about you."

She sat on the sofa and he sat next to her, still holding onto her hands. "I'm sorry about your brother." She couldn't bring herself to call Stefan her father, because he hadn't been her father. Yet when his eyes clouded over with dark sadness, she couldn't help but feel his despair.

"I loved my brother very much," Lester said. "His death came as a huge shock to all of us. There is much fear and concern here, as I'm certain there is in the vampire clan."

Lester looked to Adrian and nodded. "Is Robert faring well?"

"He's fine. Still trying to get to the bottom of what happened," Adrian said.

"As we all are. Who would want to kill Stefan? And why did Stefan suddenly wish to bring Harlee out in the open when he had hidden her for so many years?"

Harlee wished she knew the answers to all these questions, or at least knew who the real daughter of Stefan and Amelia was. She felt guilty for perpetrating such a fraud on these people, but what choice did she have? As an agent for the government, she was duty bound to do her job, which meant gathering information on the lycans and vampires. Still, she couldn't help the discomfort that accompanied her lies.

"Would this beauty be my cousin?"

Harlee peered around Adrian and Duncan to see a mirror image of Lester, only much younger.

"Harlee, this is my son, William. Your cousin."

Harlee stood and William came over to embrace her. "Welcome to the clan, Harlee."

"Thank you. This is all a bit strange."

He grinned and the room lit up. The man was extremely handsome. "I'll bet it is. I can't even imagine having your entire world changed in the blink of an eye. Can't be easy for you."

William was as warm and welcoming as Lester, making her feel relaxed and comfortable. "It hasn't been, but I'm trying to adjust."

"We'll try to make it easier for you," William said. "I don't have brothers, sisters or any cousins, so you're the first for me. I'll just think of you as a sister," he said with a grin and a wink, then kissed her hand.

Harlee caught Adrian's rolling eyes and Duncan's glare. Clearly something about William bothered them. Either that or they were both jealous that she was getting attention from another man, even if that man was her "cousin".

Something about that thought made her smile.

"Let me show you your father's rooms," Lester suggested, standing and reaching for her hand.

Harlee stood and walked with him down the hallway and up a staircase that led to a private suite. Within it was a separate apartment that Lester explained belonged to Stefan. Harlee wandered around the expansive rooms, absorbing the quiet of the wood floors, the excellent taste in art work and furnishings that Stefan collected. When she wandered into a study, she was drawn to a framed picture on the uncluttered desk. She picked up the picture of a woman who looked very much like her.

"That's your mother," Lester said.

The picture was similar to the one Robert had showed her earlier. Again that strange pang of loss, of memory, of seeing a picture of someone who looked so much like her it was uncanny. This whole story couldn't be true, could it? Wouldn't she somehow have known it, felt...different? She traced the figure of the young woman in jeans and a long man's shirt, her hair unbound and flying in the breeze of night. She appeared to be standing on a balcony.

"It was taken when she and Stefan ran off together. It's the only memory he had of her, other than a few things he kept in a locked box here." Lester took a box out of a desk drawer and handed it to her. Inside were bundled letters, now yellowed and tied with a ribbon. She ran her hand over the letters and looked up at Lester.

"Stefan and Amelia wrote poems to each other," he said, smiling. "The box also contains her hairbrush and a few of her other personal things. The box is yours now. You're Amelia's daughter and I'm sure he'd have wanted you to have it."

Harlee placed the letters back in the box and closed it, feeling the urge to shove it back in Lester's hands, knowing she had no right to these things. Intimate things between two lovers whose time had been cut all too short.

"Thank you," she whispered, feeling guilty again for letting him believe she was Stefan's daughter. These lies were getting harder and harder every step of the way.

"These mementos were all he had left of her. Other than knowing you were out there, of course."

She stared at the picture of Amelia. The photograph mesmerized her, filling her with questions she wasn't certain she wanted answers to. She placed the picture back on the desk and wandered around the room, trying to shake off the feeling of melancholy.

"That's a picture of my father and your father," William said, pointing to a painting over the fireplace.

The painting showed two young men, very similar in appearance, dressed in vintage clothing and standing in front of what looked like a castle. Had to be somewhere in Europe. Harlee stared at the painting, easily differentiating Stefan from Lester. Again, that feeling of familiarity struck her as she looked at some of Stefan's features.

They had the same chin. Or was she just imagining the resemblance between her and Stefan and Amelia? Had this whole thing taken on some kind of dream-like fantasy?

Shaking off her ridiculous thoughts, Harlee moved around the apartment. When she reached for a door handle down the hall, Duncan's hand covered hers.

"That's Stefan's bedroom."

"So?"

"He was murdered in there."

"I want to see." She didn't know why, but it had suddenly become important for her to know what had happened to him.

Duncan paused for a second, then removed his hand and allowed her to open the door. She stepped in and Duncan flipped the light switch, bathing the room in brightness.

It was easy to spot the bloodstain on the carpet in front of his bed. She shuddered then wrapped her arms around herself to ward off the sudden chill. "How did he die?"

"He was stabbed with a silver-tipped knife. Silver will kill us," Lester explained.

"And you have no idea who did it?" she asked.

"Not yet," Duncan said, "but we'll find out soon enough."

"Had to be a lycan," Adrian said. "No vamps have access to this place."

"And you know as well as we do that it could have been anyone, lycan or vampire," William said, glaring at Adrian. "We're not assuming it was a lycan. Why would a lycan want Stefan dead? It makes no sense. He was our leader."

"There are lots of reasons," Adrian said. "Maybe your father did it so he could take over."

Fury turned William's face a bright red. He advanced on Adrian, murderous intent on his face. "How dare you accuse my father of this! He loved his brother, as we all did!"

Harlee stepped back as William's eyes began to glow a bright yellow, his face distorting as it began to shift. Though she'd seen pictures of transformed lycans, they had never been able to force the transformation of any they had captured. She stood, mesmerized as long claws ripped from William's fingernails.

"William, stop," Lester said quietly, placing his hand on his son's shoulder. "Tensions are high right now and Adrian is right. We can't afford to assume a lycan didn't do this. It could be anyone."

As soon as the transformation began, it was over. William's eyes returned to their normal brown color, though the fierce look he gave Adrian made her distinctly uncomfortable. Adrian didn't seem the least bit bothered by William's rage, standing there with his arms crossed and a half smile on his face.

"You are welcome to stay with us, Harlee," Lester offered after they left Stefan's bedroom. "There is much you need to learn about your lycan side."

"Perhaps someday I'd like to do that," she said, "but right now I think I'll stay in the neutral territory of the corporate headquarters." She didn't want to appear to take sides, plus she knew that security was so high in this place she'd never be able to slip away. As it was, a contingent of guards had followed them from room to room. The idea of escape was impossible here.

"I do hope you'll come visit me there, though. I just need some time to…get my bearings and get used to this whole idea."

Lester nodded. "I understand. Plus you need to enact the changes within you and you'll need both a vampire and a lycan for that."

And that was something she had to make sure never happened, or else her life would end. As soon as they found out she wasn't a lycan/vampire hybrid, they would realize she was simply a human and kill her. She couldn't have sex with Duncan and Adrian, though she wondered if maybe the reason wasn't due to them finding out she wasn't one of them, but her discovering she really was, after all, Amelia and Stefan's daughter.

"Yes, I'll definitely need to get around to figuring all that out. Eventually. I'm in no hurry."

"But I am," Adrian whispered behind her as they made their way downstairs again.

Duncan made his way to her other side and added, "As am I."

She shuddered, the sensual promise in their voices creating an instantaneous sexual ache, awakening her mind to visuals of tangled bodies writhing together. Inhaling a shaky breath, she forced her thoughts on escape instead of passionate images of being naked, aroused and deliciously sandwiched between Duncan and Adrian.

Chapter Seven

ಐ

After having lunch and more discussions about her background, they left to head back to Dark Moon. The sun had just begun its trek toward the horizon, the late dusky afternoon giving way to early darkness.

Harlee was determined to start focusing! Enough of these ridiculous notions that she could possibly be the daughter of Stefan and Amelia. The fantasy was over. Duncan and Adrian were slowly moving in on her and weakening her defenses. If she was going to escape with her life and the information on the lycans and vampires, she had to do it soon.

Maybe a diversion while they were driving. Getting out in public would be the best place to make a run for it. At Dark Moon, she was just as closely watched as she had been at the lycan mansion. It was now or never. She casually looked out the window of the SUV, trying to figure out where the hell they were. The windows were tinted so dark she could barely make out streets and road signs. Just like on the way over, none of the landmarks looked familiar. It was as if she'd been taken to some strange city she'd never been to before, some place in another realm.

It made no sense.

And the dark SUV didn't help. No doubt they had to keep the windows darker than normal in order to protect Adrian, yet there was no sunlight today. Instead, a soft mist fell and the sky was overcast, threatening a deluge of storms.

None of the landmarks looked familiar. They'd obviously taken her out of the city the first night in the helicopter, but for the life of her nothing they passed seemed familiar. They had flown for awhile, but not long enough to leave the state, or at least she hadn't thought so. Now she wasn't so sure.

Lost or not, there had to be humans milling about, and if she could get out of the car and make a run for it, she could find help and shelter. Duncan and Adrian wouldn't dream of revealing themselves to humans.

"Duncan, this is your territory and I've only been here a few times, but I don't remember ever seeing any other cars on this route," Adrian said.

"It's pretty secluded out here," Duncan replied. "Usually anyone coming this far out is lost or taking a scenic drive. You hardly ever see any traffic this far out. Why?"

"Just after we crossed that intersection, two cars came out and they're closing on us fast. If you weren't so busy ogling Harlee in the rear-view mirror, you might notice what's happening on the road."

"Screw you."

Harlee whipped her head in the direction of Adrian's thumb. Two black SUVs were rapidly gaining on them. They looked like government vehicles. Blacked-out windows, nondescript license tags. But how would they know where to find her?

"I see them," Duncan said, adjusting the rear-view mirror. "Probably nothing, but let's keep an eye on them."

"I don't like it," Adrian said. "Something doesn't feel right about this."

"Then let's call for backup just in case something's up."

"Give Harlee your phone and have her call your headquarters while I alert Dark Moon."

Duncan passed his cell phone back to Harlee and gave her quick instructions to speed dial the lycan mansion. "Tell them who you are and let them know I said to get some men ready if we need them."

"If you want me to give location details, somebody better tell me where the hell we are," she said.

"Just tell them we're about twenty miles south of the main road. They'll know where," Duncan replied.

Harlee made the call while scooting sideways in her seat so she could keep an eye on the SUVs. They had settled into position about fifty yards behind and didn't seem to be making any attempt to close the gap. That alone made her suspicious. Plus the fact there were no other cars on this deserted stretch of road and her heart began to race.

If it was her government, what was their intent? Had they found out about the lycan mansion and followed Duncan when he pulled away?

"I've got Dark Moon on alert," Adrian said.

"Good. I've got a really bad feeling about this. We may need all the help we can get."

"Then let's get them started this way," Adrian suggested.

"Not a bad…"

Duncan was interrupted by what sounded like a loud pop in the back of the car.

"That was gunfire!" Harlee shouted.

Duncan swerved and hit the gas, but the two SUVs crept closer, the bright flash of weapons fire causing her to shrink down into the seat. She closed her eyes and waited for the rear window to break.

"This car is armored and the glass is bulletproof, lass," Duncan said, his concentration straight ahead as he maneuvered the winding road at breakneck speed. "They're gonna need more powerful weapons than that to do any damage."

Good to know. She had no doubt the average car would be swiss cheese by now.

Adrian turned around and faced her, a gun in his hand. "Get down on the floor and stay there."

Why the hell did she have to get down on the floor if the car was bulletproof? Nevertheless, she did what she was told but she didn't like it. Feeling helpless wasn't one of her favorite things to do.

Harlee inched back up to peer out the rear window when she felt the vehicle speed up. Glancing into the front, she noticed Duncan was doing well over a hundred miles per hour and yet the vehicles behind them were still closing on them.

"Call the lycans," Adrian shouted. "Tell them we're taking heavy fire," he instructed her while shouting basically the same thing into his own cell phone.

She did, at least feeling somewhat useful.

"We need to speed up if we're going to outrun them until our backup gets here," Adrian said to Duncan.

"Too many curves," Duncan said. "If I hit it too hard we'll be in the ditch."

"Why the hell didn't we fly here in the chopper or be smart enough to bring an escort?" Adrian asked.

"Well, it's too fucking late to think of that shit now, isn't it?" Duncan replied, swerving as they careened around a curving patch of road.

The lead chase car had closed to within a few feet of them now, but for some reason, they had ceased firing at them.

"They've stopped shooting," she said. She wondered why.

Her answer came seconds later when the vehicle rammed them. She lurched forward and crashed into the back of the front seat, grabbing onto it for support. Duncan somehow managed to keep them on the road despite swerving back and forth across both lanes.

"Shit!" Adrian said. "They're trying to drive us into the ditch. They figured out we're bulletproof so the only way to stop us is get us off the road!"

Harlee peered over the top of the back seat just in time to see the vehicle behind them pull even with their left rear quarter panel and swing into them, clipping them and causing their car to swerve violently.

"Fuck! I'm losing speed!" Duncan said, trying to control the vehicle.

"Harlee, can you see anyone?" Adrian asked.

"Two people in the front of each vehicle," she said. "Can't make them out though. They're wearing black baseball caps and sunglasses. White males."

"I see someone in the back seat of one of the vehicles too," Adrian added. "They sure brought a big party with them."

Not that she would know every government agent, but she didn't recognize the men in the vehicles.

They weren't going to make it before help arrived. She knew it, could tell they weren't going as fast as they were before.

Finally, Duncan regained control and floored the accelerator, seemingly pulling away from the vehicles chasing them.

"We're pulling away again!" she said, watching more and more distance appear between their car and the others. "Maybe they're going to give up!"

The two vehicles behind them had pulled side by side now. Harlee saw someone leaning out the window of one of the vehicles. A bright flash appeared and she held her breath as their vehicle rocked from the force of an explosion hitting the road next to them.

"Shit! That's why they backed away! That was a fucking rocket! They must have some light anti-tank weapons or RPGs or something. Hold on!" Adrian yelled, reaching for Harlee and pulling her over the seat, tossing her underneath him and covering her with his body. Something detonated beneath the car, the impact knocking the breath from her. Another rocket! Their vehicle went airborne and she slammed against the dashboard. The only thing saving her from tumbling around like clothes in a dryer was Adrian's strong grip holding her in place. She heard the rushing whoosh of the airbags deploying.

Her equilibrium in ruins, she held on as the vehicle turned over and over, finally coming to rest on the driver's side. Pain shot through her rib cage as she tried to move, her breath somehow stuck in her abdomen. All she could hear was a slow hiss like air escaping from a tire. Smoke filled the vehicle, making her cough. God, her stomach hurt. She needed to throw up. Her entire body felt battered and she could hardly move. But a tiny voice inside her screamed *get the hell out of the vehicle*.

And Adrian no longer held onto her. Scrambling to a sitting position and fighting the dizziness and nausea, she looked out where the windshield used to be and saw they were in some kind of tall grass. She could see Adrian positioned on his belly, pistol aimed toward the road, but couldn't figure out where the hell Duncan was.

Before she could move to crawl out the window, Duncan snaked an arm around her middle and dragged her out of the car, literally tossing her to the ground. She hit with a thud and caught her breath, tucking her arms around her as she rolled a short distance and stopped near Adrian, who grabbed her and pulled her close to his side.

"Know how to fire a weapon?" he asked.

She nodded and he pulled a pistol from his waistband and thrust it at her.

A Glock, she was grateful that it was at least familiar. God, how long had it been since she'd been to the firing range? Too damn long. And her hands were shaking, the aftereffects of the rolling vehicle taking its toll on her nervous system. Steadying her hands, she cocked the weapon, placed the butt in the palm of her left hand and aimed in the same place Adrian was looking. Duncan positioned himself to her other side, drawing a weapon of his own.

"We'll never hold them off," Adrian said. Harlee looked at his grimacing face, realizing they'd never escape this.

The only thing keeping them from discovery right now was the thick smoke from their damaged vehicle.

"We're screwed," Duncan said.

Harlee bit her lip, wanting to leap up and flag down the government, tell them to stop shooting, that she was human. But then what? Duncan and Adrian would be taken, or even worse, killed on the spot. Her stomach rolled at the thought.

When the smoke cleared enough to see the black SUVs, Harlee spotted at least four men, weapons drawn and searching the smoke-soaked field for them.

But she couldn't see faces, couldn't tell who they were, only shadowy bodies, though they seemed to be looking right at her! One drew his arm back and threw what appeared to be a canister of sorts in their direction. An explosion of white light turned night into brilliant day, temporarily blinding them.

"Sonofabitch!" Adrian shouted. "They're using light laser grenades!"

Suddenly the sound of buzzing exploded near her ear as bullets whizzed past near her. They used the light to begin firing on them!

Duncan and Adrian began firing back as a spray of both bullets and bright laser fire flew at them.

God, what kind of weaponry were these people firing at them anyway?

She heard Duncan grunt but had no time to see what he wanted. She aimed her weapon and fired, peppering the ground in front of the SUV with bullets. Instinct spurred her to defend her life. She couldn't think about the fact she was firing at her own people, though she was careful to aim in front of them, not at them. They didn't know she was there, and short of standing up and waving her arms around, they weren't going to know. She wasn't about to be shot trying to identify herself, and despite the mixed emotions it caused, she wouldn't put Adrian and Duncan in jeopardy.

All three of them fired nonstop, Adrian tossing her another clip when she went empty. But the others had more firepower, the smoke was rapidly clearing and soon they'd be sitting ducks again.

Just then the whirring noise of an approaching helicopter and the screeching tires of fast-moving vehicles captured her attention. Through the haze of smoke she saw the men jump into their vehicles and go speeding off.

"It's Dark Moon security!" Adrian shouted, then half-stood in the tall grass and looked overhead. The whistling sound of a descending rocket made her cover her ears. The impact of the explosion rocked the ground underneath her. When she looked up, she saw a ball of flames where one of the black SUVs had been.

"The others are taking off!" Adrian shouted, then took out his cell phone to make contact with the helicopter, instructing his men to chase down the remaining SUV. It whirred off in a hurry.

Adrian rushed toward the road, yelling at Harlee to stay put. She did as she was told, too confused and dizzy to want to move. Instead, she laid her head on her arms and fought for control over her breathing. When she managed her riotous emotions, she looked up to see the road clear with the exception of two bodies lying on the ground and an SUV engulfed in flames.

"It's all clear!" Adrian shouted. "Let's get out of here!"

"Let's go!" she said to Duncan, urging him with her elbow as she stood. But when she turned around, he was still face down on the ground. Panic sent her heart hurtling to her stomach and she dropped beside him. "Duncan, are you hurt? Can you hear me?"

No response, no movement. She turned him over, searched his body looking for a wound, reaching underneath him until she felt the warm, sticky wetness at his abdomen.

Shit! With as much care as she could, she turned him over. Bright crimson spread from his chest to his midsection. Despite her shaking hands and upset stomach, she ripped the shirt away, using it to clear away the blood.

The wound was huge, and near his heart! Quickly balling up the shirt, she pressed it hard to his chest to staunch the flow of blood, not daring to leave his side to go for Adrian. But it didn't take Adrian long to come looking for them. His eyes widened when he caught sight of them and came running down the slope toward her.

"What happened?"

"He's been shot or wounded in some way. I can't tell whether it's a bullet or something else."

Adrian took a close look at the wound, his face grim as he met her gaze. "The bullets were probably laced with silver. Otherwise he wouldn't be down. We have to get him back to the lycans. They'll know how to care for him."

And just where the hell were the lycans anyway, Adrian wondered. They were much closer to lycan territory than vampire, and even with Dark Moon using the chopper the lycans should have arrived first. So where the fuck were they?

The answer came seconds later as six dark SUVs appeared around the curve and came to a screeching halt. Lester and William flew out of the lead car and ran over. Adrian hurried up to meet them.

"What the hell happened here?"

"Not now. Get your man down there to pick up Duncan. He's been shot and there's silver on the bullets."

Lester signaled for four of his men to retrieve Duncan, but he and William stayed with Adrian. "Now explain what happened."

Adrian dragged his fingers through his hair. "I have no fucking idea. Someone followed us from the mansion and shot at us."

William's eyes narrowed. "Government?"

"Maybe. I'm not sure. Couldn't tell from their vehicles and haven't gotten a close look at them yet. Two are in the ditch over there," he motioned. "Let's go see who they are."

They were interrupted as Duncan was carried up the slope and placed into the back of one of the lycan vehicles. Harlee came running over, her hands covered in blood. Duncan's blood.

"I...I want to go with them," she said, a noticeable tremble in her hands. "Make sure he's okay."

Her eyes glittered with unshed tears, etched lines of worry creasing her forehead. Adrian nodded and she turned and climbed into the vehicle carrying Duncan. His gaze lingered on the spot long after the car drove away, then he mentally shook his head to clear the visions of her. There were more important things to focus on than Harlee and her decision to go with Duncan. Hell, he didn't much care for lycans in general, but Duncan was one of the few he considered a friend. Then again, he knew more about lycan recuperative powers than she did, so maybe she needed to see it for herself. Though he'd rather she'd stayed with him.

For her own protection, of course.

Turning away from the quickly disappearing car, he strode over to William and Lester. "Let's go catalog this mess," he said.

"Why don't you go back to Dark Moon and report what happened," Lester said. "William and I will stay behind to clean up this mess."

"I don't think so. I need to see who these guys are."

"Our men already looked," William said. "Not lycan or vamp. You can smell the human all over them."

"We have things under control," Lester added. "Dark Moon needs a report. Take care of that, Adrian."

Shit. He hated losing control over this. Something wasn't right, but Adrian had neither the time nor patience to fight the burly-looking lycans standing guard over the scene. The chopper reappeared and he shrugged and headed toward it.

His gut told him something was amiss, but he had no idea what it was. He had plenty of time to think about it though. And after he finished giving the report to Dark Moon, he'd head back to the lycan mansion to check on Duncan and Harlee.

He really needed to talk to Duncan. Questions had arisen. Serious questions that his mind refused to let go of. Maybe Duncan would have the answers.

If he survived.

After several hours explaining what happened to Robert, who also had no idea how the government had found them, he pulled out his cell phone and dialed Duncan's number.

No answer. He tried the main line at the mansion and the lycan who answered said Duncan was resting. Lester and William were also deemed "unavailable".

What the fuck did that mean? Was Duncan in a coma or sleeping? Was he dead and the lycans refused to tell him? They wouldn't bother to go look for Harlee either.

Goddamit. He'd have to go back there and figure out what was going on, obviously the only way he was going to get answers.

And figure out where Harlee was and what she was up to. Grabbing his keys, he headed toward the garage, mentally cursing when he ran into Sara. She stood there wringing her hands with a worried expression on her face.

"What's up?" he asked.

"I'm worried about Harlee."

"I'm going to check on her now. And Duncan. I'll let you know what I find out."

"Oh you are? Good, I'll go with you. Robert wanted me to talk to Lester about some business anyway."

Shit. The last thing he wanted or needed was Sara tagging along. "Can't you do this later? I don't think they're up for business after what happened today."

She lifted her chin. "That *is* the business I'm going there to discuss. Are you leaving now? I can be ready to go in five minutes."

The day had just grown progressively worse.

Chapter Eight

ဢ

"It's all right, lass. It'll heal soon enough. Just weakened me for a minute."

Weakened her ass. Duncan had been bleeding so hard he could have died within minutes. "We almost lost you."

"If the bullet hadn't been coated in silver, I wouldn't even have flinched. I was lucky it passed through me. I'll be fine."

Fine. If she heard that word again she'd scream. She felt impotent, unable to do anything but sit there and watch him rest in bed. Something Duncan apparently didn't do very well. He fidgeted every few seconds and scowled incessantly. She tried to keep him in place by talking to him.

"How do you think the government found us?"

He shrugged. "Don't know. But I'll be looking into it."

She refused to admit how frightened she'd been. Her fear hadn't been for her own life, though, which surprised her. She feared what they'd do to Duncan and Adrian when they caught them. Harlee surmised whoever had been chasing them wasn't the least bit interested in capturing them. And that scared her more than anything. Scared her, and made her angry. After all, the government's goal was to eliminate the lycan and vampires completely. Elimination meant killing.

And they'd almost killed Duncan. Between the ultraviolet laser fire and the silver-coated bullets, it was obviously their intent to kill both the vampire and the lycan.

"I'll be all right, lass. Just give me a few minutes to recover."

"Few minutes my ass, Duncan. You almost bled to death."

"Trust me. I'll be fine."

There was that word again. Even though the lycan physician had insisted Duncan would heal, she couldn't imagine a gaping hole like that just closing up.

"You're very pretty when you worry," Duncan said.

Harlee looked up and met his gaze. There was at least some color in his face now. And he was smiling. Grinning, actually. "I'm not worried."

"Yes you are. You're worried about me. I take that as a compliment, lass."

"Just don't want you dying," she muttered, feeling embarrassed about worrying so much about him. He wasn't even pale any longer.

"Harlee, look at the wound."

She approached the bed and sat next to him. When he lifted the sheet away from his chest, she was surprised to see the wound had already closed and was healing, only a light pink scar left.

"Lycans heal quickly."

"But those bullets had been laced with silver." And she knew that silver was lethal to lycans, just as ultraviolet light was to vampires.

"Aye. That's why the healing didn't take place right away. But the bullet passed through me so quickly it didn't have time to deposit much, if any, of the silver."

"Won't silver kill you instantly?"

"Not necessarily. Depends on how long the silver's within us. If it's embedded, then within minutes. If the bullet had stayed, the silver would have dissolved and entered my bloodstream. I'd be dead already."

"That's what happened to Stefan?" she asked, certain her eyes were playing tricks on her as she glanced at his wound. It was almost completely healed. She sighed in relief even as she stared at it, wide-eyed with disbelief.

"Stefan was stabbed with a knife dipped in liquid silver. As soon as it went in the silver entered his bloodstream in its liquid form and killed him within minutes."

She had so much to learn about lycans, and an equal amount about vampires. But for the moment, she was grateful Duncan had escaped death. "I'm glad you're going to be okay."

"Why, thank you, lass," he said, cupping the back of her neck and shocking the hell out of her by pulling her toward him.

Too curious to resist, she allowed him to bring her closer. His tongue snaked out and traced her mouth, then slid past the seam of her lips and touched hers. Energy surged at the first stroke of his tongue to hers, a lightning strike centered low in her belly. Heat pooled between her legs and her libido came to raging life. She whimpered against his mouth and threaded her fingers through his thick, silky hair.

In a swift move, he grabbed her waist and dragged her on top of him. She pulled back, shocked and worried about hurting him. "Duncan!"

"Darlin', I have to feel you against me. Now shut up and kiss me."

"We shouldn't do this." For so many reasons, the least of which was that someone could walk in, though the fire raging in her blood made even that possibility a weak threat.

"You spend way too much time thinking," he said, making the decision for her by kissing her and shutting her up. This time, his tongue wasn't gentle when he plunged it inside her mouth. He wrapped his arms around her and pulled her against his chest. She grabbed for his arms, appreciating the hard, thick muscles under her hands.

Another hard, thick muscle rubbed against her pelvis, and Duncan rocked it against her. She whimpered at the sweet sensation of his thick cock caressing her clit, visualizing what Duncan had done to Annmarie last night on the dance floor. His huge hand had dwarfed Annmarie's pussy as he petted her clit, leisurely bringing her to climax. Harlee could already imagine the feel of his hand against her sex, coaxing an orgasm from her. He was so big, everywhere, from his hands to his arms to the thick shaft pressing against her. Something about a man so huge appealed to her in a primal way she couldn't begin to fathom.

She might not understand it, but she felt it, visualized it, imagined his big body covering hers, his huge cock plunging between her pussy lips and filling her completely. Her pussy quivered, cream wetting her panties. Her clit throbbed with the unspoken need to be touched in the same way he'd touched Annmarie.

When she whimpered at her conjured visuals, he growled against her lips and pressed harder, this time stroking her tongue in the same way she wished he'd stroke the knot of sensitized nerve endings between her legs.

Oh, God, she wanted that, needed sweet release instead of the driving tension that she'd lived with the past two days. Fears of death, of discovery, of what could possibly happen to her when they realized the truth, had consumed her every waking moment.

Didn't she deserve a moment to play, just a little? She wouldn't have sex with him, that could potentially reveal too much. Or too little as the case may be. But Duncan's mouth was warm, the movements of his tongue oh so seductive, his hands roaming in a careless, lazy rhythm that lulled her into total relaxation and yet drove her into a near frenzy at the same time.

His lips were impossibly full, soft and perfect as they languidly drifted across hers. She could kiss him for hours and be content. But then one hand swept over her breast and rested there. She felt the heat of it sear her skin through her clothing. Her nipple puckered and a sharp tingling sensation spread throughout her body. A very pleasurable tingle.

Maybe just kissing *wouldn't* be nearly enough.

Duncan kept his eyes closed and listened to the sound of Harlee's breathing. Rapid, like her ever increasing heartbeats. The scent of her filled the room. Sweet, musky arousal, her perfume dove into his senses like a heady, irresistible drug. He wanted to be inside her. Now. His own breathing grew harsh and labored as he moved his hands over her buttery soft skin. Her nipple grew harder against his palm, the soft globe so fragile under his hand as he petted the distended bud.

She moaned. He liked the sound of that, so he did it again. She arched into his hand and he opened his eyes to savor the vision of her. Her face was flushed, her eyes shut tight, her lips parted as she drew in a ragged breath.

"*Brèagha*," he whispered, and she opened her eyes, taking his breath away. She really was incredibly beautiful. Such innocence and curiosity in her eyes, something Duncan wasn't accustomed to with women. He didn't know how to handle her, afraid she'd crumble under his touch.

Desire glittered in her eyes, sparkling like a perfect emerald. A woman like Harlee needed to be cherished, protected and loved like a princess.

He wasn't that man and he knew it, but he also knew if he didn't taste her, if he didn't bury his cock deep inside her and join with her at least once, he'd regret it forever.

Holding tight to calm reserve, he resisted the urgent need to thrust inside her and pound away like the animal he was. He rolled her off him and onto her back then took her mouth again. He could kiss her forever, her lips sweet and compliant, their taste like tender fruit. Her nipples beaded against the thin halter and he covered one full mound with his hand while thrusting his tongue deeply in her mouth. She met him with equal fervor, tangling her fingers in his hair to hold his mouth against hers, her hips moving against his in silent invitation.

An invitation he wasn't about to pass up. Though he controlled the beast within him, it threatened to burst free, intent on ravaging the red-haired beauty under him. That he could not allow, sensing she wasn't ready to see the "real" Duncan. For now he'd have to be content to love her in human form.

But damn it was difficult!

Harlee fought the sensations coiling inside her, but it would have taken a saint to deny how good this felt. She wanted this. No, she needed it. Aching tension tightened every muscle, and something weirdly biological was going on inside her. The urge to fuck was strong—much stronger than anything she'd ever felt. She had to have Duncan soon or she was afraid she'd have a total meltdown.

First thing she needed to do was get these clothes off. His naked chest brushed her erect nipples, but the halter was in the way. "Please," she whispered, pushing at Duncan's chest to move him off her. He rolled onto his back and she scrambled to her knees, reaching for the ties at her neck. Duncan kept his gaze trained on her, watching every movement of her hands with a hunger that fed her sense of urgency as she freed the ties of the halter, then let it drop to her waist.

His eyes darkened, his chest rising as he breathed in a deep gulp of air. But he didn't reach for her. Instead, he slid his hands behind his head and watched her, letting her take charge.

Strange, she'd never stripped for a man before. As she reached for the waistband of her skirt and pushed it over her hips, she realized how wanton, how sexy she felt. She was in control and this huge, powerful man was letting her lead. Arousal pounded between her legs, cream trickling down her thighs. Her thoughts ran rampant as she watched Duncan snake his tongue across his bottom lip, imagining how it would feel if she straddled him and let him lick her throbbing pussy.

The ache intensified. Shuddering with need and anticipation, she wriggled out of her skirt, slipped off her panties and climbed on top of Duncan, both shocked and aroused at her boldness. He seemed equally surprised, his eyes widening before narrowing into a half-lidded, sensual look that tore her up inside.

It wasn't like her to be this aggressive with sex but she couldn't help herself. Something deep inside her drove her to distraction, compelled her to take instead of hold back. She wasn't even supposed to contemplate having sex with Duncan. This wasn't good.

Oh, but his cock felt so fine. She moved against him, sliding her wet pussy against his shaft, dragging her clit against his hardened flesh. She felt the contractions deep inside, felt the moisture increase and whimpered because he wasn't in her yet.

"What are you waiting for, lass?" Duncan asked, his voice a strained whisper. "Take it."

Harlee burned at his words. Unable to hold back despite the warning voice in her head telling her she shouldn't do this, she lifted, reaching for his cock and positioning it at the entrance to her pussy. His cock head was like fire as it made contact with her slit.

A momentary hesitation made her pause. She searched Duncan's face and found only acceptance and patience within it. If she stopped right now, he wouldn't press her further. But the thought of not seeing this through, of not feeling him inside her, made her ache with a sense of loss. There was a power waiting for her she wanted to experience, something new she had to explore and she couldn't resist.

Consequences be damned. She wanted this. Leaning over to capture his mouth with hers, she slid down his shaft. He groaned into her mouth and grasped her buttocks in his hands, spreading them apart and helping her settle on top of him.

Magic. Devilish magic. His cock pulsed as her pussy gripped tight around it. When he pushed deep, she cried out against his mouth and he thrust his tongue against hers.

Oh, God this felt so good. He felt so right, so perfect inside her. Strong, powerful, showing no weakness from his injury. Relief mixed with pleasure as he drove deep, gripping her ass and maneuvering her up and down his shaft.

"So tight," he muttered against her lips, his tongue snaking out to draw a light touch against the tip of hers. Sparks of pleasure shot between her legs, her pussy pouring her juices over them both.

She couldn't think through the sensation of heavy arousal jetting through her body like a rushing drug. She rocked against Duncan's pelvis, dragging her clit against the base of his shaft as he pulled back. Orgasm hovered close, shocking her with how fast it was all happening. She wanted to hold back. At the same time she wanted to follow that rush to its inevitable conclusion. A soft whimper escaped her lips, the tension building to unbearable levels.

"Shh," Duncan whispered, gripping her hips and pushing her deep against his pelvis. "That's it, love, ride me." He thrust his hips upward, his cock seeming to lengthen and thicken inside her. Caught in the maelstrom of a storm she couldn't name, she could only watch in shock as his eyes turned from blue to a golden yellow and his face began to change, shifting into something harder, the planes and angles of his cheeks hollowing as he underwent the transformation from human to lycan.

Mesmerized, she couldn't tear her gaze away from his face, feral lust spreading across his features. She half expected to blink and find herself straddling a wolf, but whatever changes burned within him stopped.

"I won't shift," he said, his voice hoarse and guttural, as if he fought his own lupine nature. "Let's just do this as humans. Now fuck me hard, Harlee. Draw the cum from me and drench my cock with your cream."

She half expected to change with him as a burning pain inside her intensified, but then it passed and all she felt was this incredible pleasure, this journey to ecstasy. His cock head rubbed that sweet spot inside her and the dam burst. She cried out and ground against him as rush after rush of intense pleasure sizzled throughout her body. Her breath caught and she held on tight, riding him faster and faster as if she were running away from the incredible sensations. When the tremors subsided, she collapsed against Duncan's chest.

He continued to move against her with slow deliberate strokes, and in a matter of minutes she was ready to go again. Lifting her head, she met his teasing smile.

"We're not even close to be finished yet, lass."

No wonder she liked Duncan so much. She grinned and kissed him, more than ready for round two.

Adrian kept his thoughts to himself as he stood in the foyer of the lycan mansion despite wanting to tell the idiots exactly what he thought.

What a bunch of fucking assholes. The animals who guarded the front door must keep their brain cells in constant wolf mode, because all they could manage were noncommittal growls when he said he wanted to see Duncan. They informed him Duncan was busy but when he felt up to it he'd come downstairs and meet with Adrian. Sara had already bounded away intent on searching out Lester so she could discuss the ambush with him. Adrian thought about following, but he needed to see Duncan first and he wasn't about to wait for the morons to inform Duncan he was there.

So he sat in the library, sipping coffee and appearing bored and uninterested in the activity around him. It didn't take long for the gorillas to forget he was there. Once they left, so did he, taking the stairs and heading toward Duncan's room, intending to tell him exactly what he thought of the imbeciles who guarded the gates of hell. At Duncan's door he reached for the handle then stopped when he heard a low moan.

A low, female moan, followed by whispered words spoken by a very familiar voice.

Harlee.

Instant irritation boiled his blood at the thought of Harlee in bed with Duncan. Why the idea of her fucking his friend bothered him he didn't even want to think about. It was what it was. Jealousy. He immediately forced his anger away and turned the knob, inching the door open a crack.

Harlee was naked on top of Duncan, her taut buttocks tightening as she moved forward and back against him. Her head was tilted back, her hands kneading her own breasts. Hardening in an instant, Adrian fought to keep his hand from straying to his own cock. Despite his ridiculous jealousy, he was turned on at the sight of her fucking his friend. How easy it would be to step into the room, pull his shaft out and slide it between the cheeks of her ass, burying himself in the heat of her firm backside.. His balls tightened painfully, but something kept him from going in there and doing exactly what he'd been told to do. He and Duncan were supposed to fuck Harlee together, to urge her blood to rise to the surface and free the lycan and vampire within her. But goddamit, he was pissed off and had no desire to do what he was supposed to do right now. He had no intention of getting his dick within miles of Harlee. She'd decided who she wanted to fuck and it wasn't him.

God, she made him crazy. Jamming his fingers through his hair and pulled the door shut. When he turned to leave, Sara was standing there, a wicked grin on her face.

"I had no idea you were so into voyeurism," she said, reaching out to trail one long fingernail down his chest. "It's quite a turn-on, isn't it? Makes you want to fuck, to feel what they're feeling."

"I thought you were meeting with Lester," he said, ignoring her comment.

"I'm finished and he had another meeting so I came looking for you." She took her other hand and cupped one of her own breasts, the nipple clearly outlined against the thin silk of her blouse. "And here I am, watching what you were watching. It made my pussy wet, Adrian. It made me want to fuck."

Fucking Sara had long ago lost its allure. Nevertheless, he was just annoyed enough to take what she so obviously offered. Right here, right now. He grabbed her shoulders, turned her and pushed her back against the wall, then leaned against her, grinding his cock between her legs. Her lips parted and she gasped, lifting her skirt and pumping her pelvis against his.

She wore no panties, the golden hairs of her pussy glittering with some kind of dusting powder. Her scent screamed her arousal, her need clear as he watched her canines extend.

Sara had wanted the bite of intimacy, of mating, since the first time he fucked her. He always withdrew his fangs before he passed the point of claiming her. Fucking her had been a fun pastime. Keeping her would be a lifelong sentence of misery.

And right now all he wanted to do was fuck. He slid his hand between her legs, cupping her sex. Moisture spilled onto the palm of his hand and she closed her eyes and moaned.

"Fuck me, Adrian. I need it."

So did he. The problem was, the woman he wanted to fuck was currently riding his friend. The woman he wanted to be inside of had another cock buried in her. The woman he wanted was Harlee.

"Shit." He removed his hand and backed up a step. Sara's eyes flew open in shock.

"Why did you stop?"

"I'm not in the mood."

Her gaze traveled to his crotch. "Bullshit. You're hard as steel and ready to burst. You're hot, you're horny and so am I. So fuck me."

"I don't think so."

When he turned away and headed toward the stairs, she followed, grabbing his arm. "What the fuck is wrong with you? You've never turned it down before."

"Well, I did now. I've got things to do."

"Oh. I see how it is. You want that bitch in there."

One thing about Sara that always bothered him was her assumed claim on him. Since the first time he'd fucked her she thought they were mated, that they'd always be together. Despite all the times he'd told her all they had together was sex, she refused to believe him, insisting he'd come around to her way of thinking some day. "Sara, I don't think it's a good idea for us to have sex anymore."

"Because you want Harlee," she said, her lips forming her expertly practiced pout.

"No, not because of Harlee. Because I'm tired of the way you hound me, the way you cling to me like you've got some claim on me. When I decide to take a mate, it'll be one I choose, not one who assumes she's mine because I stick my dick in her. I've got to get back."

But Sara barred his way, her chin lifting, her eyes glittering with anger. "I refuse to be dismissed, Adrian. You and I have something together, we always have."

"Only in your mind." Moving around her, he started down the stairs, knowing how Sara's games worked. She wasn't finished with him yet, and wouldn't be until she got the last word in. As he opened the front door and made his way out, she yelled after him.

"You fucking bastard! You'll come crawling to me eventually!"

Shaking his head at her pathetic whine, he headed to his car, intent on blowing away the disasters of the day with a stiff drink.

Maybe several.

And then, maybe, just maybe, he could forget the vision of Harlee fucking anyone but him.

Chapter Nine

ဢ

Lying there on Duncan's chest, listening to the rhythmic sound of his heart beating against her ear, Harlee was content. Duncan's wound had completely disappeared and based upon his earlier performance, it was quite obvious he'd made a full recovery.

He'd been amazing, taking her to new heights of pleasure. She should be ecstatic, exhausted and ready to pass out. Instead, she felt this weird angst, a vague sense of urgency. Something compelled her to get back to Adrian.

Why she thought about Adrian right now made no sense at all. Sex with Duncan had been amazing. He was a tender lover, not at all what she'd expected based on what she'd witnessed between him and Annmarie. She'd expected an animal, and what she'd gotten was much different. In fact, she'd half expected to feel some kind of physiological changes within her, almost believing that she was part lycan.

Would that have made her life easier, or more difficult? She didn't know, and felt a little ridiculous that she'd expected some kind of monumental transformation. She was, after all, completely human. But Duncan hadn't exhibited any surprise at her lack of alteration, so she kept quiet about it.

She wasn't all that certain how she felt about the whole sex thing with Duncan. It was thrilling, of course, but she wasn't sure if she felt good about it or just plain guilty.

Then again, why in hell should she feel guilty? She was a grown woman able to make her own choices about sex, about whom she slept with. She had no ties and no attachments, so who had she betrayed by sleeping with Duncan?

Adrian?

Preposterous. He was nothing to her. They'd played a little at the club and that had been it. Though he'd made dark, exciting promises to her, telling her exactly what he'd planned to do to her, she had no more relationship with Adrian than with Duncan. She was a free spirit, a woman who could choose any lover, or lovers, that she wanted to.

Smiling, she realized she liked having that kind of power. So the guilt trying to hammer her insides could just go the hell away. She wasn't interested in feeling bad for what she'd just done, and that little voice clearly needed a nap.

"I suppose I should get you back to Dark Moon now," Duncan whispered, kissing the top of her head and running his palm down her bare back.

She snuggled against him and lifted her head to look at him. "I kind of like it here."

He smiled. "Lass, you're welcome to stay with us. With me. That's entirely your choice. I just assumed you'd want to get back there. After all that happened today, I'm sure Robert is worried and I know Adrian is probably going crazy wondering about you. I'm surprised he didn't show up here."

Her eyes widened at the thought of Adrian bursting into the bedroom to find her riding Duncan's cock. Would he have been shocked? Disgusted? Or would he even have cared? Maybe he'd have been turned on.

Maybe *she'd* have been turned on knowing he watched. Her nipples beaded into tight knots, her sex awakening with a tiny tremor of renewed arousal.

"I think you're right. It's time to go back."

It was time to stop thinking about things she shouldn't be thinking about. Things she didn't *want* to think about. Her life was screwed up enough at the moment without wondering what the hell her heart was thinking.

Duncan sent her back to the vampire mansion with a driver and several lycan bodyguards, informing her he was going to remain behind overnight in order to talk to Lester and William about the attack. He promised to join her tomorrow and kissed her passionately before releasing her at the front door. The taste of him still lingered on her lips, the scent of him on her body. When she arrived back at the mansion it was late and no one was around downstairs to talk to her. Good. She wasn't in the mood for conversation. She headed up to her room, intending to take a quick shower and slip into bed, hoping for one night of complete oblivion.

Adrian stood just outside her door, leaning against the wall with his arms crossed and an irritated glare on his face. He dismissed the lycan bodyguards who had accompanied her, the tension emanating from him so thick she could slice through it.

Okay, he was pissed. About what? "Hey," she said.

He didn't answer, just stepped into her room behind her and closed the door.

"Duncan's going to be fine," she said, confused by her own feelings of awkwardness.

"I know. He called me after he sent you back here."

She wondered what else Duncan said but wasn't about to ask. Instead, she walked into the bathroom and grabbed a towel from the closet, then turned to find Adrian standing in the doorway.

"What are you doing?" she asked.

"Guarding you."

"I hardly think anyone will slip into my bedroom and slit my throat while I'm sleeping. I'll be fine. I need to take a shower and get some sleep."

"Exhausting night?" he said, challenge in his voice.

Too damn tired to deal with whatever kind of mood he was in, she said, "Yes. It's been a hard day. I was shot at, Duncan nearly got killed. Hell, we all nearly got killed. Pardon me if I find that rather exhausting, so if you don't mind, I'm going to shower and go to bed and I don't need a damn bodyguard standing over me."

"Really," he said, arching a brow and sitting on the edge of the bathtub. "And when did you become an expert on assassination?"

"I'm not in the mood for this, Adrian. Honestly, I'm tired and I'd really love some privacy."

"Seems to me you didn't need privacy last night at the club. No privacy there when I made you come. I don't think you're at all modest, so cut the act."

Her face flamed but she refused to take the bait. "Have it your way then." She untied the halter and let it fall to her waist, then slid it and the skirt off and turned on the shower, refusing to even turn around and look at Adrian. Let him look, or glare, or whatever he wanted to do. She stepped into the shower without a backward glance, keeping her eyes closed as she washed her hair and rinsed it, then scrubbed her body from head to toe. When she opened her eyes, she could see his dark outline, still sitting on the edge of the tub.

Something about him watching her was exciting, even though she knew all he could see was her shadowy form. As she rinsed her body, running her hands over her bare skin, every nerve ending stood on edge, screaming for her touch, especially the ones connected to her nipples and her clit. If she touched herself, would he enjoy watching? Would he join her?

Did she want him to?

Hell yes she wanted him to. Her pussy was throbbing in anticipation, the need to feel his cock inside her stronger than any urge she'd ever felt. Her breasts tingled and she could already envision him stepping naked into the shower and covering her body with his hands and mouth. How it would feel, how he would taste when he kissed her. She moved her fingers between her legs, caressing the tight knot of nerve endings, letting the moan escape freely and hoping like hell she wasn't making a supreme ass of herself.

Adrian watched the movements through the frosted shower door. He could only see Harlee's shadow, but he knew damn well what she was doing. Christ, was she trying to kill him? His cock tightened and engorged quickly as desire spread through him like unchecked wildfire. How easy it would be to strip and step in there with her, taking what she so clearly wanted him to take. He palmed his cock through his jeans, watching the sultry movements of Harlee's body as she turned her back to him and swayed her hips in a seductive dance.

The pulse of his cock pounded against his hand. He reached for the top button of his jeans and popped it open, then grabbed the zipper.

"Go for it, cousin."

He whipped around to find Annmarie standing in the doorway, a huge grin on her face. Turning to Harlee, he realized she had her head under the water and didn't hear Annmarie come in.

"What are you doing here?" he asked.

"Just popping in to see Harlee, but if you're going to have a little action I'll wait 'til later."

Christ, couldn't a guy get a break around here? "You watch her for awhile. I'm tired of playing babysitter."

"You sure about this? I don't think babysitting is what you had in mind just now."

"Fuck off, Annmarie," he said, brushing past her and heading toward the bedroom door. He needed to get the fuck out of there and clear his head. The last thing he needed right now was to fuck a woman who pissed him off so badly he forgot what she'd done earlier today. And with whom.

"Love you too, Cuz," she laughed after him.

Harlee was tired of waiting for Adrian to make the first move and get his ass in the shower with her. She was waterlogged and damned near deaf from the water splashing over her. It was time to shut off the water and throw open the door, come out stark naked and see what happened after that. Her body was pulsing and ready and by God she needed him. After wringing out her hair, she took a courage-inducing breath and pushed the door open.

Her jaw dropped when she saw Annmarie sitting on the tub where Adrian had been. She blinked, unable to speak.

"Not quite who you were expecting, honey?" Annmarie said, a quirk to her lips.

"You surprised me."

Annmarie handed her a towel. "Yeah well, so did my cousin when I stepped in here and found him just about to drop trou. Sorry 'bout that."

So, he was thinking about joining her and just suffered an interruption. Well damn. Still, she smiled. Was it possible to be happy and frustrated as hell at the same time? "No problem." She finished drying off and slipped on a long T-shirt. Annmarie followed her into the bedroom and they both flopped on the bed, staring up at the ceiling. "I don't understand him."

Annmarie snorted. "He's a man. Of course you don't."

"He seemed really pissed off at me tonight, but I can't figure out why."

"Did you two argue about something when you were at the lycan mansion earlier?"

A cold shadow passed over Harlee. "The lycan mansion? Adrian wasn't there."

"Sure he was. He and Sara took a drive out there. Sara had to meet with Lester, and Adrian went to check up on Duncan and pick you up. You didn't see him?"

Oh, God. That's it. No, she didn't see him, but she'd bet anything he saw her. With Duncan.

"No. I...didn't see him."

"Hmmm, were you too...busy?" Annmarie said with a cocky grin.

Harlee shot a glance at Annmarie, wondering how she'd feel if she told her about what happened between her and Duncan. She'd seemed really into him at the club last night. Maybe Harlee had stepped in territory she shouldn't have.

Shit.

"Something's on your mind," Annmarie said, sitting up and criss-crossing her legs. "Tell me."

Harlee sat too, facing Annmarie. "You might not like it."

"Try me."

"It's about me and Duncan," she said, biting her lower lip in anticipation.

"You fucked him."

Unable to read Annmarie's expression, Harlee nodded. "Yeah."

Brow arched, Annmarie's lips curled into a knowing smile. "Bet he was good. Tell me everything and don't spare the details!"

Harlee expelled the breath she'd been holding. "Oh, thank God! I thought you'd be pissed."

"Why would I be? I don't own Duncan. I might like to fuck him someday, but other than that I have no interest in being tied down to one mate. Not when there are so many men I've yet to try."

"You are so bad," Harlee said, then on impulse grabbed Annmarie and hugged her. "I've never really had a confidante, someone I'd consider a friend."

"Me either. I don't like most people. They annoy me."

"Then I'm glad you can tolerate me. Your cousin can't seem to."

Annmarie waved her hand in dismissal. "Ignore him. He's just pissed off because he's hot for you and doesn't want to be."

Harlee wasn't certain if that was a compliment or not. "I think maybe he saw Duncan and me together today."

Annmarie nodded. "Probably. And I'll bet he was jealous as hell. Isn't that great?"

"Great? He probably hates me now."

"Honey, trust me. He doesn't hate you. He wants you. He feels something for you. If he didn't feel something then seeing you with Duncan wouldn't have meant a thing to him. The fact it pissed him off means something big. That kind of thing doesn't happen to Adrian and he doesn't know how to handle it." She threw herself back onto the bed and giggled. "Oh this is just perfect!" Rolling onto her side, she propped her head against her hand and said, "Now we just need to figure out how to torment him about it."

Harlee's face fell. "I don't want to torment him. I feel bad he saw what he did. Something happened today between Duncan and me. It was like a boiling, urgent need that I couldn't control. I don't know. Maybe it was just relief that he wasn't seriously injured."

"Or maybe it's the lycan half of you needing to mate."

She wished her feelings were that easy to explain. But since she wasn't lycan, there had to be another reason for her to have jumped Duncan when she'd never intended to.

"Tell me something," Annmarie said. "If it bothers you so much that Adrian saw you and Duncan having sex, then maybe your feelings are stronger for him than they are for Duncan?"

God, she hoped not. "Why would you think that?"

"Well, let's put it another way. Picture you and Adrian doing the mattress mambo together. And Duncan walks in. How would you feel knowing he was watching you?"

She pondered the thought for a few minutes then realized she was getting turned on picturing Adrian's long, lean body covering hers, his cock pumping in and out of her wet pussy and Duncan standing beside the bed, stroking his thick shaft as he watched.

"That's a damned exciting thought," Harlee admitted.

"Thought so. You've got it bad for my cousin. You have my sympathies."

She didn't know what to make of these mixed-up feelings, but she was at glad to at least have Annmarie to help. "I should go to him and explain about Duncan."

"That is the last thing you should do. Never go to a man. Make him come to you. Especially someone like Adrian. I can guarantee that thoughts of you are filling his every waking moment. You're driving him crazy. It's only a matter of time, honey."

"Until what?" Annmarie made no sense.

Annmarie smiled knowingly. "Until he comes storming through that door, rips your clothes off and fucks you until you're too weak to stand."

Dear God. Could she handle that? "I'm not sure about this."

"Trust me. It's coming. But be prepared for it, Harlee. He's pissed off about how he feels. I know my cousin. He uses women for a quick fuck and he doesn't like entanglements. He's tangled with you in a big way and he doesn't like it one bit."

Her heart pounded and her palms grew moist at the thought of an incensed Adrian crashing through her bedroom door and taking her without a single word. She'd never subscribed to the caveman dominating his woman theory, but right now the visuals bombarding her were just that. And the strange thing was, she wanted it, craved it with a need that was stronger than anything she'd ever felt.

"Someone else touched his woman, and Adrian's about to lay claim," Annmarie said. "Vampires are very territorial about their mates. When they mate, they don't share."

"Mate? I'm not his mate."

"Yeah, you are. Anyone within the vicinity can feel the vibes between you two."

Harlee shook her head in denial. "If that was the case, then why did I have sex with Duncan?"

"Instinct. Because you have to. It's part of your lupine nature to mate with a wolf. But you're also half vampire and that need is growing just as strong. Besides, my cousin gets to you, though heaven knows why since he's a rude pain in the ass."

Refusing to delve into the whys of her feelings for Adrian, she said, "That still doesn't explain Adrian. Why would he even care who I fucked?"

"Because he's already claimed you as his. He just hasn't admitted it to himself yet."

"How do you know all this?"

"I might be a brassy, loud-mouthed bitch, but I also study the nature of vampires and lycans. Trust me, the men are as primal as it gets when it comes to their women. They take, they mate, and it's for life. I know Duncan. He desired you, and obviously the feeling was mutual. We indulge our physical desires without apology, Harlee, so you have nothing to be ashamed of.

"Now Adrian is different. He wants you, but it's more than physical. You're going to have to decide pretty damn quick if it's him you want, because if it isn't you need to let him know."

Let him know? How could she let him know anything when she didn't understand herself? "I'm not sure I can. I'm so confused!" And getting more so by the minute. She might be letting them believe she was half lycan and half vampire, but Adrian was full vampire. And Annmarie wanted her to commit to Adrian? How could she do that? She was human and she didn't belong here.

What if he did do what Annmarie said he was going to do? Then what? Could she still extricate herself from this situation? Did she even want to? She dropped her chin to her chest and closed her eyes, too tired to think anymore tonight.

"You're exhausted. Get some sleep." Annmarie kissed her cheek and pulled the covers over her. "I'll tell Adrian to stay the hell out of your room and let you get some rest. You know where to find me if you need to talk."

Harlee nodded and watched Annmarie flip off the light and close the door on her way out. She rolled over and pulled the blanket up to her chin.

She didn't want to talk. She didn't want to think. She wanted to go back in time to a few days ago when her life was completely different, before it became so damned complicated.

Go to him. Don't go to him. Talk to him about Duncan. Or don't. Make love to him. Don't make love to him.

What the hell was she going to do?

Chapter Ten

20

Adrian paced the hallway, his keen sense of hearing picking up the sound of Harlee's breathing.

Typically any instruction Annmarie gave him would be ignored, but her tone when she told him to stay the hell away from Harlee tonight rang of genuine concern. And Annmarie was usually never concerned about anyone but Annmarie.

So what was wrong with Harlee? Was she sick? Upset? Pissed off?

And why the fuck did he care? Christ, the woman made him crazy. Why couldn't he just do what he needed to do with her and leave it at that? Why did he even care if she screwed Duncan? He could have joined them, gotten off and fulfilled his obligation at the same time. But no, he had to act like some moronic jealous lover and storm off.

Now his cock was still hard, his balls were tied up in knots and his frustration had reached the boiling point. The problem was, he didn't know if he was more upset at Harlee or at himself for feeling this way. And frankly, he was tired of these pent-up frustrations. Harlee'd all but offered herself to him earlier with her sexy shower dance, but Annmarie's typical lousy timing had stopped him.

Tension and frustration had mounted for the past few days. First this mess with Stefan's death, then having to rush over and kidnap Harlee, then being told he had to fuck her, then wanting to fuck her, then the attack... Christ, what a mess. Maybe if he took out his frustrations on Harlee, this constant driving need that seemed to be directed at her would go away.

Pausing in front of her door, he made his decision. Reaching out, he turned the knob on the door handle and stepped in, expecting to find the room in darkness and Harlee sound asleep. But as soon as he opened the door, the room filled with light. Harlee sat up in bed and looked at him, an expression of wary expectancy on her face.

"Thought you were asleep," he said, closing the door behind him.

She looked down at her hands. "I can't sleep."

"Why not?"

"Don't know. Too much going through my mind, I guess."

He knew the feeling. There was a reason he was pacing outside her room in the middle of the night instead of putting a guard at her door and getting some sleep himself. He approached the bed. "What's on your mind?"

She looked up and watched him. "Things."

"What kind of things?"

"I don't want to talk about it."

Talk wasn't what was on his mind either. He stopped next to the side of the bed, inhaling her scent. God, she smelled sweet. The perfume of her blood was an aphrodisiac, compelling him to dive into her neck and puncture the artery there, then drink from her until he came, hard. He wanted to change her, to bring out the beast within her.

He wanted her to be vampire. It had suddenly become important and he knew exactly why.

"Did you enjoy Duncan today?" he asked, refusing to allow himself to sit on the bed next to her. As badly as he wanted her, he was too angry, too unsettled to let himself touch her yet.

Her eyes widened for a second. "You watched us, didn't you?"

"Yes."

Her cheeks flamed pink but she didn't look away. "I don't know what to say. I feel like I should apologize for that, but why the hell should I? You and I don't have anything together."

"I didn't ask you to apologize." Though he was pleased she'd even thought about it. It meant...well, what did it mean? God, he felt like a kid with his first crush. This was ridiculous. "I shouldn't have come in. Good night."

"Hey! Wait a minute," she said, scrambling out from underneath the covers and following him toward the door. He stopped and turned to watch her progress, his gaze straying to her long legs visible underneath the T-shirt. Her nipples were hard, outlined like pebbles against the thin cotton. "What the hell is wrong with you, anyway? First you come in here like you want to talk, like you want to..."

"Fuck?" he finished for her.

"Well, yeah. But now you're leaving?"

"Yes. I'm leaving."

"Goddamit, Adrian! Quit screwing with my head!"

She had a lot of nerve talking about screwing with someone's head. "Oh, right. Like you haven't been playing a little game of your own with Duncan and me?"

Her eyes went dark and she shook a finger at him. "I have done no such thing and you know it. It's the two of you who've been pressuring me to play this three-way game of fuck-and-tell, so don't even try to play innocent. And why do you even care what I do with Duncan? You don't have any feelings for me!"

She'd said it like it was an accusation.

"Don't tell me how I feel, dammit!" This whole conversation was juvenile.

As she inched closer, he felt her cinnamon-spiced breath across his face. "And don't tell me how I'm supposed to feel, or think you can dictate who I sleep with! I've just about had it with you! I might just go and live at the lycan mansion for awhile."

"Over my dead body."

"You're already dead," she said, a smug smile on her lips as she crossed her arms over her middle.

"You watch too much television. I've never been dead."

"Well then I guess I could tell you to drop dead. So drop dead and get the hell out of my room! I've had enough of this."

She turned to walk away but he grabbed her upper arm and whirled her around. Her lips formed a surprised o.

"Enough? We haven't had nearly enough, Harlee. We haven't even started. Game's over and talking is getting us nowhere." He jerked her against him. "Let's cut the bullshit," he said, just before his lips came crashing down over hers.

He waited for her to push him away, expected her angry response. Instead, she wrapped her arms around his neck and met the thrust of his tongue with a whimper, nestling her body closer to his. She tasted like seduction, like something he needed more than he wanted to. His balls twisted in a knot of agony, his cock hardening painfully.

Christ, she felt good against him. Her heart pounded against his chest, mirroring his own erratic beats. He moved his hands over her curves, finally having her exactly where he needed her—in his arms and as eager as he was. But one thing was wrong—entirely too many clothes kept his bare skin from touching hers. He pushed her back and jerked the T-shirt over her head, then reached for her breasts, pinching the hard nubs of her nipples between his fingers. Her response was immediate, her groans audible as he rolled her nipples between his thumb and forefinger, squeezing them, pulling them.

"You like it hard, don't you?" he asked.

Her answer came in the form of a loud groan.

He had to get naked and fast. He wanted to take his time with her, suck her pretty tits, lick her from her neck to her toes and spend all night loving her, but he didn't have the goddamned patience right now.

Releasing her breasts, he jerked the shirt over his head and fumbled for the buckle of his belt. Harlee's eyes widened, but she didn't say a word, just watched while he removed his clothes then drew her against him once again.

Though he did like the way her gaze strayed to his crotch and lingered there, enjoyed the way she licked her lips like she wanted to wrap them around his cock. And he wanted them there. His cock wanted them there too, bobbing upward in response to the movement of her tongue across her lips.

Soon. But right now he wanted to feel her skin. He dipped and took her lips again, then searched her body with his hands until he found the globes of her ass and squeezed hard, jerking her against him, needing to feel her sweet pussy rubbing against his hard-on. When she met his thrusts eagerly, grinding her pussy against his cock, he groaned into her mouth.

Fuck! He could so easily lose control with her.

Releasing his hold on her ass, he grasped the back of her neck and claimed her lips, driving his tongue deep, punishing her with a kiss that ravaged, that took instead of asked permission.

She didn't seem to care. She tangled her fingers in his hair and pulled, hard. He wasn't gentle and she seemed to prefer it that way, seemed to need this pain that he inflicted on her. Was her passion as far gone as his? God, he hoped so. Wrapping her hair around his fist, he used it to spin her around and push her against the wall, her palms making contact with a loud slap. He pressed her against the wall until her forehead touched it then swept her hair to one side, revealing the tender nape of her neck.

"Remember when I asked you at the club if you liked to be bitten, Harlee?" he whispered in her ear, grinding his cock against her ass. "Remember when I told you exactly how and where I wanted to bite you?"

Harlee moaned, remembering every wicked word he'd whispered to her at the club, how he'd told her he wanted to take her clit between his teeth and tug. Her nipples tightened and cream flooded her thighs. She wanted that. Here, now, tonight, no more hesitation, no more reasons not to. She wanted Adrian and nothing was going to stop it from happening.

"Answer me!"

He tugged her hair again, his teeth scraping the nape of her neck.

"Yes!"

He bit down lightly, not using his fangs. But still, it hurt. Oh, God, it felt so good. Goosebumps popped out along her neck, her breasts ached for more of the sweet torture of his fingers and her clit was a tight knot of nerve endings begging for his teeth to do exactly the same thing he was doing to her neck.

"Tell me what you want," he commanded, his teeth so close to her neck she felt the soft scrape of them along her skin. "Tell me and I'll give it to you."

She couldn't stand this torture. His cock nestled between her legs, his hard body pressing against her. Why was he doing this to her?

"Tell me, Harlee!"

"Bite me, goddamit!"

He moved to her side, jerked her head back, met her eyes and let his fangs slide down. He bent to her throat, his tongue like fire as he licked a trail along her throat and sank his teeth into her neck. Searing pain burned at the contact.

It hurt. It tingled. And something else. Something incredible. Pleasure bubbled up like an erupting volcano. As soon as his teeth were buried in her neck, she came.

"Oh my God!"

Huge waves of orgasm had her convulsing in his arms. Good lord, she hadn't expected such pleasure. What was he doing to her? He wasn't touching her pussy, her clit, wasn't fucking her but the climax was like being struck by lightning, sparking inside her and coursing through her veins as he sucked at her throat in rhythmic pulses. Harlee clutched his arm and his back, holding tight to him as she rode out the exquisite sensations. Warm, sticky wetness flowed down her neck and onto her breasts. She felt dizzy, hot, her blood boiling as strange sensations poured through her.

When Adrian released his hold on her throat, she felt empty inside, bereft. She whimpered, holding onto him as if she wanted to beg him not to let go. But instead of feeling weak, she felt a power surging through her, strengthening her. She looked to him and he nodded, his eyes glowing an eerie red.

"It's inside you, Harlee. You can't deny it."

She didn't know what to say to that. Had what inside her? Some kind of weird chemical response to him biting her? She'd been bitten by a vampire. Holy shit. Was that why she felt these weird sensations inside? This sense of power, of invincibility? "I don't understand these feelings."

"And I don't feel like taking the time to explain them to you right now. I need to fuck you, to eat your pussy, to make you scream over and over until we're both too damn tired to talk. We'll talk tomorrow."

He grabbed her wrist and dragged her over to the bed, literally throwing her on top of it then planting his hand firmly on her belly to hold her in place. Like she'd even think of going anywhere after what he said he wanted to do with her. Despite the orgasm from his bite, need spiraled through her as if she hadn't come, as if she hadn't come in a very long time and craved it desperately.

Adrian grasped her ankles and pulled her toward him. Her butt hovered at the edge of the bed and he dropped to his knees between her legs. He rested his fingers on her thighs and pushed them open wider.

"You smell like sweet honey right here," he said, then pressed a kiss halfway between her knee and upper thigh, inching his way up.

Harlee watched, unable to keep from doing so, needing to see what she felt as he moved his mouth in a maddeningly slow pace over her flesh, stopping short of her inner thigh. His gaze met with hers just as his mouth covered the pulse point of her inner thigh.

Oh, God, he wouldn't do that to her again, would he?

He would. His fangs slid down over his eyeteeth and he bit into her femoral artery. Blood poured from the side of his mouth and she jerked once, then twice as a flood of sensation rocketed through her.

This orgasm was more intense than the first—hotter, deeper, crashing through her like a flood that had burst a dam. She bucked against his mouth, begging him to stop, pleading with him not to stop as the waves of pleasure grew with every pulse of her blood into his mouth.

And again, she felt strange, like a powerful force had entered her very soul, strengthening her, making her feel superhuman, as if she could leap from the bed and fly around the room even as the rush of her climax began to ease. Sweat poured from her as Adrian removed his teeth from her thigh and licked the wound closed then looked up at her.

Not a trace of blood remained on her leg or on his face, though it seemed as if gallons had pumped from her. She waited for him to say something. Instead, he moved to her pussy and captured her clit between his lips, sucking the distended bud between his teeth, biting down with a light nibble that sent her into the throes of ecstasy once again.

Could a woman die from too much pleasure? If so, she welcomed death willingly. "Adrian, what are you doing to me?"

"Branding you," he whispered, then licked where he had bitten, swirling his tongue around her pearl before descending lower to lap at the cream pouring from her. When he slid his tongue inside, she tilted her head back, closed her eyes and groaned. His tongue was long, hot and utterly magical, doing wicked things to her body, promising even more amazing things to come.

He lapped her from her pussy to her clit, stroking her to another blinding orgasm. She shrieked, lifting her hips to grind her pussy against his face. He held onto her bucking hips, forcing her to hold still while he laved her cunt with relentless strokes. God, she couldn't take anymore!

"This is torture!" she cried.

"You like torture."

His voice was tight, barely controlled restraint evident in the low, husky tones. He grabbed her wrist and hauled her into a sitting position, covering her mouth with his cum-soaked lips. She tasted the tangy flavor of her cream all over his face, heard him moan when she licked at her own juices.

He tangled his fingers in her hair, wrapping them around his fist again, then pulled his mouth away and flipped her over onto her belly.

"You have one fine ass, Harlee," he said. "I'm going to fuck it one day."

She shuddered at the promise in his voice, trembled when his palm caressed her buttocks, cried out when his hand came down with a sharp swat to her cheek.

"Ow, dammit!"

"You like that."

She did. Asshole. Despite the burning sting, her pussy quaked with the need to feel his cock buried deep inside her while he did that. Why did he bring out such violent need within her? This wasn't like her at all.

When he did it again, she moaned and backed up against him, undulating her ass against his rock-hard cock. At least he groaned in response, giving her some satisfaction that he was just as affected as she was. He reached between her legs and caressed her slit, then replaced his fingers with his cock, wetting his cock head with her pussy juices. His fingers dug into her hips and he nestled against her, rubbing his shaft back and forth against her slit.

Harlee tensed, waiting for his cock to enter her, but he teased her, drawing it back and forth, then stopping.

She sighed.

"Want something?" he teased.

She wouldn't say it. Wouldn't beg for it. What a prick!

"Tell me what you want, Harlee."

Fuck you, asshole.

"Tell me!"

Whack! Another hard slap on her ass! God that felt good.

"Fuck me, Adrian! Goddamn you, you know exactly what I want!"

He shuddered against her then drove in to the hilt. She cried out, his thick shaft filling her, stretching her. The pleasure was exquisite. She'd never felt anything like it before, this utter joining as if their bodies had been made to fit each other. Her body was on fire from the inside out, just as it had been earlier when he'd bitten her.

"Tell me what you feel," he urged, pumping fast and hard.

"On fire. It's burning me, Adrian."

"Good. Go with it."

Go with it? She felt like she was dying! This pleasurable pain was unbearable! "I...I can't!"

"You can. Endure it. You have to!"

He leaned over her back, sweeping her hair to the side and sinking his teeth into her neck again. Only this time she didn't come, this time it was like a narcotic, taking away the burning pain, relaxing her so that all she felt was the pleasure. She rocked against him, pushing back against his cock, spreading her knees further apart so that she could take him deeper.

"More," she grunted. She felt like an animal, lifting her ass higher, needing him to crawl inside her and fuck her harder.

He still had hold of her neck and he growled against her, the sound vibrating against her throat. She shivered, feeling it all the way to her toes.

"I'm going to come, Adrian!"

He growled again, thrust hard, shuddering against her. She felt the moisture and heard the animalistic cry as he pumped his cum inside her. She let go then, her climax roaring through her, shaking her to the core with its intensity.

Tears stung her eyes and blinded her, gritting her teeth as wave after wave of bright light shot through her. What were these feelings that were so clarifying yet so confusing? How could she feel pleasure and confusion at the same time?

Chapter Eleven

ഌ

Harlee fingered the tiny puncture wounds at her throat, barely evident this morning. And yet they made her feel as if she somehow…belonged to Adrian.

Like she wore his ring. Or a hickey. She giggled then turned her head to see if she'd awakened him. He still slumbered like a dead man. Or undead man. Or whatever he was.

She'd slept a little. Very little, spending a lot of time simply enjoying being wrapped up in his arms and feeling utterly possessed by him and astounded by the depth of feeling she had for him.

He infuriated her. He was an arrogant, uncommunicative, infuriating, domineering pain in the ass.

She might be falling in love with him. A *vampire*. And what was she? Was she human? Or was she really what they thought she was? These strange sensations she'd felt couldn't possibly be her changing, could they? For the first time, she wasn't so sure anymore and she didn't know whether to be scared or confused or thrilled.

Wasn't that a kick in the ass?

Shifting just a bit, she turned over onto her back and stared up at the ceiling, watching the gray light of dawn enter the room while she ticked off all the reasons she could possibly be in love with him.

Top of the list was lovemaking. No doubt it was incredible, more than she had ever imagined it could be. Her blood literally sang in her veins last night. She still felt that zing inside, that strange awakening, similar to her time with Duncan, only more intense. Could her emotions have anything to do with her dominant side, or was she just feeling more for Adrian right now because lovemaking with him had been more recent?

Could she be more confused? She wasn't exactly experienced in juggling multiple lovers. How was she supposed to handle this?

She froze at the sound of the door opening, caught between not wanting to move and shaking Adrian awake. But the room had grown light enough that she immediately recognized Duncan and relaxed, especially when he smiled and put his finger to his lips to keep her from speaking.

He crept to her side of the bed, leaned over and pressed a soft kiss to her lips, sliding his tongue in her mouth to swirl with hers. Warmth curled in her belly, a banked fire slowly coming to life. All too quickly it was over and he pulled back, smiling and smoothing her hair away from her face.

Well, that was certainly pleasant. His hands circled her throat, his thumbs caressing her chin.

"I could kill Harlee with one squeeze of my hands, you fucking idiot," Duncan said, though it was obvious he wasn't talking to her.

"I knew you were here the minute you entered the house, lycan," Adrian said without turning around. "You smell like a wet dog." Adrian flopped around to face them both, arching a brow and glaring at Duncan. "You already had your turn. Get your hands off my woman."

Duncan frowned. "Your woman? I don't think so. Besides, you keep fucking her and passing out, she'll be dead in no time. You can't even stay alert enough to protect her."

"I told you I knew you were here." He pulled Harlee close to his side.

Duncan grabbed her arm and dragged her to the other side of the bed. "Bullshit. You didn't even flinch. You don't have the first clue how to protect her."

When he pulled her over to his side of the bed, Adrian nearly pulled her arm out of her socket this time. "I wasn't the one lying near death yesterday. How the hell are you supposed to protect her when you're dead?"

Harlee felt like a rag doll, her irritation growing with every passing second. "Excuse me, but I'm not a war prize here." Jerking her arms away from both of them, she scrambled to the end of the bed and grabbed her T-shirt, tossing it over her head. Resting on her heels, she cast a disapproving look at both of them. "You're both acting like a pair of testosterone overloaded teenagers. Instead of trying to figure out who gets to fuck me next, why don't you work together to figure out who was trying to kill us? Maybe it's the same people who tried to kill Stefan."

They both looked at her with raised brows. "It was the government."

"So the humans killed Stefan."

"Didn't say that," Adrian mumbled.

"Then maybe you'd both better start thinking with something other than your dicks, because as long as I've been here you've gotten nowhere, and yesterday we almost died. Let's get with the program, fellas."

Robert listened at the door and smiled. Harlee was so much like his sweet sister Amelia it was uncanny. The looks of a demure kitten but the fire of a tigress. Harlee was coming into her own, feeling her bloodlines boiling. Soon it would be time for her to make her choice, to determine her dominance. He knew all it would take was some time alone with both Adrian and Duncan, and it appeared she had mated with both of them. Now she had to take them both at the same time.

If she ended up dominant lycan, it would benefit the vampire clan because she had already bonded with them. If she ended up dominant vampire, she would be his link to his sister and would rule at his side, eventually taking over the reins of the vampire nation.

Ah yes, it would all happen soon, but first her dominance needed to be determined and that might require a little boost in the right direction. Things weren't happening nearly fast enough in that department. He pushed open the door to Harlee's room, pasting an angry look on his face.

"The two of you have failed to protect my niece," he said, casting an angry glare toward Adrian and Duncan.

"She's fine," Duncan said.

"We hadn't expected the ambush," Adrian said, slipping on his boots. "Besides, why would the human government want Harlee dead? They don't even know about us."

"Are you certain of that?" Robert walked past the two men and pressed a kiss to Harlee's forehead. She smiled up at him.

"Hell, I'm not certain of anything anymore," Adrian mumbled. "I'll look into it today."

"No, you will not. I'm concerned about Harlee. I want her removed from the mansion and taken to a neutral, safe territory until we determine who was behind Stefan's murder and the attack yesterday. We don't know if it was lycan, vampire or human. The only people I trust are the two of you and the immediate family, and there are too many others here or at the lycan mansion that we cannot be certain of."

"Where do you suggest?" Duncan asked.

"The cabin. No one outside the family knows about it. You'll be safe there."

"What's the cabin?" Harlee asked, wondering why they had to change locations.

"It's like a fortress," Robert said. "High on top of a mountain, views from all four sides, very remote. Impenetrable and highly secure. You'll be safe there with Duncan and Adrian."

Would she be safe? Or would she be prey? And was she concerned about that, or excited?

She wasn't sure.

"I'll shower and pack a few things," she said, turning away from the two men staring so intently at her.

The cabin was amazing. They'd helicoptered in, landing high on top of a snow-capped mountain peak. The air was cold, the skies crystal clear. The facility was more like a one-story mansion, with floor to ceiling windows surrounding the entire structure. Bulletproof, Adrian assured her. At the bottom of the steep slope was an electrified fence and a gated guard shack. No one was getting up here without a fight.

She felt completely safe and totally isolated.

The refrigerator was well-stocked and Adrian was outside gathering wood for the stone fireplace while Duncan opened a bottle of wine. The sun was setting in a blazing display of orange as it drifted behind a giant white cloud. She felt like an angel sitting on top of the heavens being catered to by a couple sexy satyrs. Not a bad way for a girl to spend an evening.

Steaks were cooking on the indoor grill, the sizzling sounds and incredible smell tantalizing her. She sat back on the couch and tucked her bare feet under her, surveying the dark-paneled living room.

A thick rug had been placed in front of the fireplace like one of those scenes she'd seen in an old movie. She could already picture herself sipping a glass of champagne in front of a roaring fire while lying naked on that plush, furry rug. A winding staircase led to an open bedroom that overlooked the living room. The kitchen was expansive with shiny chrome appliances and enough food to last at least a week. She kind of liked the idea of getting snowbound here with these two.

Funny how her life had changed in such a short period. She still didn't know what had caused the abrupt change in her perception of lycans and vampires, but instinct told her these people were not the savage killers the government had led her to believe. There were still so many things she didn't understand about all this, she had to take it all one step at a time, and first was finding out if she really was who and what Robert said she was.

And that meant she had to have sex with Adrian and Duncan. She'd like to think she was merely resigned to the inevitable, but frankly she was damned excited about the prospect, which was strange as hell considering she just realized she was in love with Adrian. How could she love one man but want to have sex with another?

She'd become a slut.

How fun!

"What are you smiling about?" Adrian asked, kicking the door closed with his foot.

She looked up at him and grinned. "Oh, nothing."

"You have something evil on your mind."

He had no idea. She felt so restless and edgy, as if something monumental was about to happen. Adrian started a fire and Harlee helped Duncan prepare dinner. They sat and ate, the room so quiet she could hear them chewing. She wondered if they were thinking the same thing she was, though she couldn't tell by their appetites. They ate voraciously, while she could barely eat a bite, especially with them watching her like beasts awaiting feeding time.

After dinner, she curled up on the couch and stared into the fire, watching the flames lick higher and higher with each log Adrian fed into the fireplace. The room warmed, her body heating so much she slipped off her shoes and sweater.

And still, the room was quiet. When she turned away from the fire, she realized they both still stared at her, Adrian from his spot on the hearth and Duncan from the chair next to the couch.

"What?" she asked.

Adrian arched a brow. "What?"

"That's what I said. You're both staring at me as if you expect me to transform right in front of you."

"That won't happen. We have to fuck you first. Together."

Leave it to Adrian to be so brutally honest. "I realize that. I think. I don't know. How is it supposed to happen? I suppose we should start with the details."

"You mean insert Peg A into Slot B?" Adrian asked.

"No, smartass," she replied. "I meant what's supposed to happen to me."

"Takes all the fun out of it if we tell you," Duncan teased, standing and approaching her.

Adrian followed suit and her heart sped up. She felt like a cornered rabbit with nowhere to run and wasn't sure she wanted to run anyway. They stopped in front of her and held out their hands, so she placed a palm in each of theirs and allowed them to lift her to a standing position. She felt dwarfed between these two large men and fought to maintain her normal breathing. Could she really handle this?

"Now what?" she asked.

"How about we just relax a little?" Adrian suggested. "You've got a panicked look on your face. Let's take a bottle of wine out to the hot tub."

That sounded like a really good idea. In theory, this whole ménage idea sounded exhilarating, but when faced with the reality of it, she wasn't certain she could handle it. While Duncan went to the kitchen to grab a couple bottles of wine, Adrian searched out an ice bucket. Harlee undressed and slipped on a robe, then waited for them at the back door.

Adrian opened the door and they stepped out into a glass enclosure that seemed suspended in mid-air. All she could see was darkness, the moon, clouds and the other mountains.

"Breathtaking," she murmured, stepping toward the glass.

"Yes, you are," Adrian replied.

She smiled but didn't turn around.

She heard the pop of a cork and the sound of wine pouring into glasses, but she was so mesmerized by the view she didn't want to leave her position.

"Harlee, come on," Duncan urged. "You can't put this off forever."

Reluctantly, she turned around and faced two sets of expectant faces watching her. Always watching her, as if she held the key to some great mystery. She didn't even know what it was she was supposed to know or do yet, only that something was supposed to happen when she made love to them tonight. Something beyond the monumental experience of making love to two men at once, as if that wasn't enough. It was for her, at least.

"I don't know what to do," she admitted, feeling rather virginal in an odd sort of way.

Adrian pulled his shirt over his head and unzipped his jeans, letting them fall to the floor. God, he was already hard, magnificent with the moonlight shining on his body. He stepped over to her and untied the sash of her robe, drawing it off her shoulders and letting it fall to the floor. "Just let it happen naturally, baby," he said. "Nobody's in a rush here, okay?"

He pressed his lips to hers, so uncharacteristically patient he surprised her. She nodded and let him lead her by the hand to the edge of the hot tub. Steam rose off the water, issuing a silent invitation to her tense muscles. She held onto his hand while she stepped in and settled down in the relaxing warmth. Adrian followed her into the water then she turned and watched Duncan undress, observing for the first time the subtle differences between the two men.

Duncan was hairier. She wondered if that was because he was a werewolf. She giggled.

"What's so funny?" Duncan asked as he straddled the edge of the hot tub and slid down the side.

"You're hairier than Adrian."

He reached for a glass of wine and settled in. "That's because I'm manlier."

"In your dreams, dog-boy," Adrian said, downing his first glass and reaching for the bottle to pour another.

"You're just jealous because you don't have the testosterone levels I do," Duncan teased.

"I don't know how you could have any testosterone with that pencil dick between your legs," Adrian quipped.

Harlee rolled her eyes, but between the warm water and the teasing banter between the two men, she began to relax. The past week she'd come to realize that despite the way the two men taunted each other, they really were friends. Which would make what was about to happen much easier than if they were mortal enemies.

"It's snowing," Adrian said, reaching behind him to hit a switch.

"It is? Really?" A soft whirring sound made Harlee look up. Her jaw dropped as the roof began to retract and small flakes of snow began to fall into the water.

"Thought you might like that. A little chill with the heat in here."

"Ohh!" she exclaimed, excited at the prospect of snow, something she'd rarely seen where she lived. She placed her wine glass on the bench outside the hot tub and kneeled in the center of the tub, tilting her head back and sticking her tongue out to try and catch the sparsely falling snowflakes, almost losing her balance several times and dipping under the water. Adrian and Duncan held onto her hands and supported her, content to let her play like a child for a few moments.

But then she caught their gazes on her, on the way her breasts bobbed in and out of the water, her nipples appearing and disappearing from view, and knew that they weren't the slightest bit interested in the cold snowflakes dropping on the steamy water and melting instantly, or catching the cool flakes on their tongues.

They were interested in her. It was time to stop stalling, to stop playing around as if what had to happen didn't need to happen, because it did. She had to see if she really was part vampire, part werewolf, or if it was all bullshit.

And if it was all bullshit, then what? Would they kill her instantly, would her love for Adrian mean nothing? Would she admit to them she was a government employee, that she had interrogated the people they had sought to find and release?

"You're thinking again," Adrian said, his brow arching. "Quit that."

She laughed. "I'm not supposed to think?"

"Not tonight," Duncan added. "Tonight just feel. You have to let it go, lass. You have to stop analyzing and just let your body relax."

Duncan pulled her onto his lap, the water making her buoyant so she straddled him easily, her knees resting on either side of his crotch. She looked to Adrian, who lazily sipped his wine from across the hot tub as he watched. She searched his face for any sign of jealousy and found none, not sure if she was upset by that or relieved, then gave up and just decided to enjoy the feel of Duncan's hands skimming along her back.

"Relax, Harlee," he urged again, his huge hands pressing inward on the tight muscles on either side of her spine.

She closed her eyes and leaned into his hands, letting his fingers perform magic on her. The snow fell in soft pellets on her breasts and face as she tilted backward, her hair skimming the top of the water. Soon she felt Adrian behind her holding her head and upper back while Duncan moved to her belly, his fingertips light despite the massive size of his hands. She'd always thought the way he touched her was incongruous with his size, always expecting him to be savage instead of gentle. It seemed as if he held back with her, treated her with deference as though he feared she'd break if he let loose.

She wondered what he'd be like unleashed, thought about asking him, but then his hands moved from her belly to her breasts and she lost that thought entirely as his palms covered her breasts, the rough calluses heightening the sensations as he scraped her nipples into screaming awareness. He squeezed, still more playful than rough, but enough that he had her undivided attention, especially when he began pulling at her nipples, each stroke sending lightning strikes of intense pleasure to her pussy.

And all the while Adrian held her back, cradling her head against his shoulder. He nipped her earlobe. Was it to let her know he was there too? She wasn't certain but how could she possibly forget about his presence? Even with the pine and outdoors filling the small room, the scent of him had become an integral part of her. She could never be unaware of him.

He bit down on her earlobe and she shuddered, arching her back, thrusting her breasts into Duncan's hands. Moving his hands onto her hips, he pulled her from Adrian, lifting her onto his lap. His cock was hard now, the wide head appearing out of the water as he adjusted his position between her legs.

Would they fuck her now?

"Not yet baby," Adrian said in answer to her unspoken thought. "We haven't even warmed up yet. This is going to be a long night."

Chapter Twelve

Duncan raised himself out of the hot tub and sat on the edge. Adrian swept her around away from Duncan, to face him. He cupped the back of her neck to draw her mouth to his. She sighed and sagged against him, needing to feel this oneness with him, this reaffirmation of her feelings for him before they moved onto the next phase of their journey.

She had no idea what she was doing. Part of her wanted to beg Adrian to take her away so she didn't have to do this, but a part of her was drawn to Duncan in an inexplicable way that made her want to turn around and draw him next to her too.

She loved Adrian, but she wanted them both. In a way, her heart was connected to Duncan, she just didn't have an explanation for it.

God, could she be more confused?

Adrian pulled back and smiled at her, understanding in his half-grin and nod. "Babe, don't sweat it. This is something we all have to do. Duncan and I don't share our women, believe me. And the last thing either of us want to do is share you. But we'll do it, just this once, because none of us have any choice."

He seemed to be able to read her hesitancy and concern. She nodded, then he turned her around toward Duncan again, pressing his chest against her back to whisper in her ear. "Now move over between his legs. I want to watch you wrap your sweet lips around Duncan's cock and suck it. Because if we're going to do this, then we're going to do it well."

Desire flared hot between her legs, his words sparking visuals she couldn't deny turned her on. Knowing he wanted what she wanted made it even more exciting.

She moved toward Duncan, watching his eyes change from bright blue to an almost storm-heavy grey, like the snow-filled clouds above them. Duncan held out his hands as she approached, reaching under her arms to pull her out of the water and capture her mouth, devouring her lips in a kiss that seared her down to her toes. Her nipples scraped the crisp hairs of his chest as he held her suspended in mid-air while he ravaged her lips, plunging his tongue in and out of her mouth the way she wanted him to fuck her. His hard cock pressed against her belly, evidence of his need for her.

He groaned against her lips, traced them with his tongue, cursed when he broke the contact of their kiss. Then he slowly slid her down his body, letting her hands rest on his thighs so she was still partially submerged in the water, her face aligned with his magnificent cock. She needed no further urging than the proximity of her mouth to his shaft. She wrapped both hands around his thick member and guided the flared head to her lips, focusing on his face as she covered the tip with her mouth. A tangy pulse of pre-cum oozed from his cock head as she sucked him against her tongue. His half-hooded eyes rolled into the back of his head and he groaned, jerking his hips forward and propelling his cock further into her mouth.

Such power she held, pleasing him this way. Cradling his balls in one hand, she stroked his shaft with the other, guiding his cock deeper into her mouth, enjoying the suction sounds, the cold snow falling on her top half and the hot tub water on her bottom half. Adrian swept his hands over her hair and down her back, cupping her buttocks then moving behind her to cradle her ass cheeks in his hands. She moaned against Duncan's cock and he growled in response.

"I love the way you suck me," Duncan said, his voice tight with strain. "The look on your face, like you're enjoying what you do. Darlin', I could shoot a load of cum deep down your throat right now just watching that look of rapture on your face."

His words curled her toes. That, and the way Adrian squeezed her ass, the way he teased her anus by flicking his finger up and down between her butt cheeks. God, she had no idea she was so sensitive there.

"You like that?" he asked, pausing to tickle that tight spot.

She released Duncan's cock from her mouth enough to moan and murmur a resounding, "Yes."

"You know I'm going to fuck you there tonight, don't you, Harlee?" He emphasized the location by pushing past the tight muscles of her anus with the tip of his finger. The tissues grabbed his flesh and surrounded it. She'd never felt anything so wholly incredible in her life. Her pussy spasmed and she could have come right then had something been inside her pussy at the same time.

Something like Duncan's cock.

Wow.

She shivered at the thought of Adrian's long cock deep in her ass while Duncan was simultaneously buried in her pussy, but she couldn't answer him, could only envision what would come later.

"Duncan. Pull her up onto the bench."

Duncan grasped her wrists and hauled her out of the water, laying her on her back on a towel he'd draped over the wide bench. Adrian climbed out and lifted her legs so her feet were planted flat on the bench, then kneeled in front of her.

"Spread your legs for me baby," he instructed.

She did.

"Wider. Let me see that pretty pussy."

Sucking her bottom lip between her teeth, she drew her legs apart even wider, mesmerized at the sight of him diving down between her legs, wondering if he'd bite her clit again.

"Do you want me to?" he teased.

"Do I want you to what?" she asked, wondering if he was actually reading her mind or if he too remembered the last time.

"Bite it again."

"Yes," she whispered, almost feeling ashamed that she did want to feel his teeth nibbling there. God, she was so different now than she'd been before, so much wilder, freer. Was that because of the lupine and vampire blood within her, or was she still as human as she'd been before, her sexuality simply blossoming under the tutelage of these two men?

That, she supposed, remained to be seen.

When his teeth scraped her clit, she lifted her hips, desperate to feel more of that tingling pleasure. When he bit harder, she moaned and closed her eyes, reaching down to stroke his soft, thick hair. His tongue snaked out and licked along her folds, diving inside to lap the juices pouring from her. Then he began to suck in earnest, leaving no part of her sex untouched.

Duncan turned her head to the side and slipped his cock between her lips, sliding inch by inch inside her willing mouth. She sucked him greedily as he pinched and pulled her nipples.

Then she felt something strange, and struggled when Adrian moved lower, and lower still. Oh, God, what was he doing? Surely he wasn't going *there* with his tongue?

But he was, and she was dying of embarrassment. She wanted to pull away, to tell him to stop, but Duncan pumped vigorously into her mouth and wouldn't let her go.

"Let him do it, baby," Duncan said, reassuring her and thrusting his hips forward. "Fuck, that's hot."

He was licking her asshole! Oh, God, that felt so good! No man had ever done that before. Hell, no man had ever gotten near *there* before. She'd never even considered it a viable option, then again she'd never been this open and eager with a man before. Now? Now she'd do just about anything.

But this? This she hadn't considered. His tongue was hot, the tip hard as he plunged it inside the dark recesses of her ass. The sensations were indescribable! And he used his hand to rub her clit at the same time, making her pussy cream all over the place.

Now she didn't want him to stop, mortified at her own behavior as she lifted her ass and pushed her anus against his tongue, wanting more of the dark, wicked pleasure. He kissed and licked her there for a long time, using his fingers to pleasure her cunt with hard, driving thrusts, his other hand to rub her clit. The sensations drove her over the edge and she sucked hard on Duncan's cock. He cursed and held the back of her head, pumping his cock so deep she felt him hit the back of her throat.

"I'm going to come down your throat, darlin', if you keep sucking me like that. Is that what you want?"

Her eyes flew open and she made eye contact with him, saw his tightly drawn expression, and nodded. She wanted him to come when she did, wanted him to experience the same satisfaction she did. He wrapped a handful of her hair around his fist and jerked her head back then thrust hard, pulling back and tunneling faster.

Adrian increased the swirling motions of his tongue against her ass, burying three fingers in her pussy and strumming her clit faster and faster until she groaned against Duncan's cock. Duncan cried out something in Gaelic and tensed, his cum shooting into the back of her throat. She swallowed greedily as a blinding orgasm overcame her. Her hot fluids poured onto Adrian's face as he kept up the motions of his fingers and tongue. Bucking against him, she tried to catch her breath while Duncan held onto her head and shuddered through his climax, then released her so she could ride out her own. She lay there, gasping for breath while Adrian moved from between her legs and stepped from the room.

Unable to move, she curled up on the bench and closed her eyes until the room stopped spinning. Dear God, that had been intense. Duncan laid her head in his lap and stroked her hair and her breasts. She heard the door open and close again and looked up to see Adrian had returned again with another bottle of wine. He opened it up and poured three glasses. She sat up and took a glass, then leaned over and kissed him when he sat next to her.

"Thank you," she said.

"For what?"

"Another new experience."

He grinned. "It's only the beginning, babe."

And still, she felt...human. Rather disappointing, actually. She'd expected something to happen by now and it hadn't.

Adrian probably expected something to happen by now and it hadn't for him yet, either. His cock still sported a rather impressive hard-on, while she and Duncan had both come. She stared down at it and pondered how to deal with his...problem.

"I want to feel your mouth wrapped around my cock now. Make me come the way you did Duncan."

"And it's my turn to taste your pussy," Duncan said, licking his bottom lip.

Her womb did flip-flops. God, would she survive the night?

Adrian stood and Harlee shifted toward him. "On your knees. I want to feed my dick to you."

God, that made her hot. Everything he said to her made her hot. She got on her knees and Duncan maneuvered on his back between her legs, only his head visible to her.

"Sit on my chest, lass, get comfortable."

She did, then she tilted her head back to make eye contact with Adrian, smiled up at him, and reached for his cock while Duncan grabbed her hips, pulled them down and fit his mouth around her pussy. The heat of his lips seared her flesh and she gasped at the sensation then licked at the head of Adrian's cock, capturing the mushroom-shaped head between her teeth and teasing him.

"Christ!" he said, reaching for her head and grasping it, then pumping his cock between her oh-so-willing lips. She twined her tongue around the broad head of his cock, flicking over it like a teasing snake, mimicking the movements of Duncan's tongue against her distended clit. The salty taste of his pre-cum dripped onto her tongue and she licked it up, demanding more with each flick of her tongue. She wanted to give Adrian the same sensations Duncan gave her, and licked along the underside of his cock head, then teased along the slit as Duncan did. She withdrew and traced the ridge along the underside of his shaft, capturing his balls in her mouth while she stroked the shaft with her hand.

Adrian held on to her head and murmured his approval with guttural sounds of pleasure.

Sucking first Duncan and then Adrian gave her a chance to compare the two men. Duncan's cock was thicker, Adrian's longer, both men tasting as different as they looked, but both like a night of delicious, dark sin. She reveled in her power over them, her control as she held them captive in her mouth and took them to ultimate release. Just as she did now with Adrian, taking him higher and higher, his balls tightening as she held them in her hand while she inched his cock into her mouth, sucking him deeper and deeper. She squeezed the sac gently, swallowing and humming while she sucked him all the way to the back of her throat.

"Fuck, Harlee!" he cried, then pumped vigorously, tightening his hold on her while he ejaculated down her throat. She shuddered, swallowing his cum while she ground her pussy against Duncan's mouth, concentrating on the movements of his tongue and controlling her own pleasure until she came in a crescendo of cries and collapsed. Rolling off him, she fought for breath and strength, certain she couldn't take anymore tonight.

And still, she was completely human. Nothing monumental had happened…well, other than two rocking orgasms and the sweet taste of the two men she cared most about. She rolled over onto her back and stared out at the stars, realizing the snow had stopped, then looked around to find Duncan on one side of her, his legs dangling in the water, and Adrian on the other side. She smiled at both of them.

"I've had enough of the hot tub," Adrian said. "Let's go inside where we can stretch out a little."

She nodded and grabbed her robe, following them in. Adrian hit the button to shut the roof, shutting out the brilliant stars above and the night that had grown so chilled she had begun to shiver despite the heat the men had generated within her.

Adrian held the door while Duncan and Harlee walked in, then shut it behind them and headed into the living room to set the bottles of wine down on the table next to the fireplace. He glanced at the clock, surprised to realize they'd been at it for over two hours already. It was uncharacteristic of him to take this long with sex, yet for some reason it had become important not to rush this tonight. Instinct told him that a threesome wasn't something Harlee was accustomed to, nor was this really something she wanted to do, even though she had slept with both of them already. He didn't want to make this a fast fuckfest that didn't mean anything.

It might be a requirement that he and Duncan take her in order to bring out the lupine and vampire within her, but that didn't mean it had to be a quick, down and dirty event. And he knew Duncan felt the same way. They had to make it good for Harlee. Hell, he'd been in a ménage before, more than once. Typically he got his pleasure any way he could, using the woman in many different ways, disregarding her needs entirely.

It wasn't going to be that way tonight. Tonight was about Harlee, about her pleasure, and he'd make damn certain it was good for her. More than good.

Why he cared about that he didn't know and really didn't care to analyze.

"Hungry?" Duncan asked.

Harlee nodded.

"I could go for a bite," Adrian added.

"You can always go for a bite," Duncan quipped.

Harlee snorted and slipped onto the thick rug in front of the fireplace, appearing completely relaxed now. Good. That's the way he wanted her. He sat down next to her and poured a glass of wine, handing it to her. She accepted it and took a sip, then leaned in to press her lips to his.

God, she tasted sweet. Of wine and something he'd never tasted before. Something he couldn't name. New? Was that what it was? She was new, poised on the verge of discovering who and what she was, and he tasted that on her? Whatever it was, he liked the taste and licked it off her lips, then slid his tongue inside to gently sip a little more of it.

Duncan came back with a plate of cheese and fruit, lifting a slice of cantaloupe from the plate and holding it out for Harlee. She bit into it and the juice ran down her chin, neck and between her breasts. Adrian followed the trail with his tongue, leaning in to capture her nipple in his mouth. She leaned back on her elbows and let Duncan feed her mouth while Adrian fed on her breasts.

It worked well for him, since all he was hungry for was her.

And he liked watching the movements of her mouth. It made his dick hard. He liked the way she sank her teeth into the slice of cheese, enjoyed the way her cheeks puffed in and out while she chewed, liked watching the undulation of her throat muscles while she swallowed a drink of wine.

She was a goddess, her body flushed with heat and arousal, tempting both of them into erections that pulsed with need, the scent of animal passions filling the air around them.

"Harlee."

She looked up, innocence mixed with elemental seductress. "Yes."

"I'm ready."

Harlee inhaled, the scent of him filling the air. "I know."

"I'm going to fill every hole you have tonight. Do you know that?"

Her breasts ached from where he had kissed them earlier. "Yes."

Adrian leaned in and kissed her, his tongue touching hers so gently she whimpered. He pulled back, and Duncan took her mouth, licking at her tongue with an urgency that made her groan.

"Harlee," Duncan said, his voice rough with need.

"Yes, Duncan."

"I need to fuck you, darlin'."

She reached for his face, her palm caressing the rough stubble of beard along his jawline. "I know."

"Suck my cock, Harlee. I ache for ya."

Adrian positioned her on all fours and got behind her, and Duncan sat and spread his legs. She bent down on her elbows and nuzzled Duncan's crotch, loving the crisp, musky scent of him. She licked the length of his thick cock while Adrian positioned himself behind her, grasping her hips and rubbing his cock head against her slit. Sparks of intense pleasure shot deep into her womb as he teased her clit with the soft head of his cock. When he parted her folds and eased his shaft inside her, she took Duncan's cock in her mouth and sucked.

Arousal deepened as Adrian nestled closer to her backside, his strokes still gentle while she was sucking on Duncan's cock.

"She's amazing, isn't she, Duncan?" Adrian asked, pulling back and thrusting again.

"Aye, that she is." Duncan rimmed the bottom of her lip with his thumb. "Such a hot little mouth."

"Such a hot pussy too," Adrian said.

Tiny quakes pulsed inside her, electrifying her with shocks of need, she moaned against Duncan's cock, and he popped it out of her mouth and lifted her chin to meet his gaze. "It's time, darlin'. I can feel it burnin' inside me."

She had no idea what he was talking about, but she felt a burning inside herself too. A burning need for completion, for something she didn't understand.

Whatever it was, it was different than what she'd felt before, and it was urgent.

Adrian withdrew and she whimpered, turning around to search for his cock, needing him inside her.

"Soon, baby," he reassured her. "Relax while we get in position."

She didn't want to relax. She needed fucked and she needed it now. She was on fire. Something wasn't right. "I'm hurting, Adrian."

"I know." He caressed her back, holding onto her while Duncan stretched out underneath her. "Climb onto Duncan. Get your pussy onto his cock, baby."

Need ran rampant through her, and she hurriedly straddled Duncan's hips, sliding over his distended cock and impaling herself on it. She screamed as he entered her, painful pleasure making her tilt her head back and howl like an animal.

Oh, God, whose voice was that? So guttural, so unlike her own.

"Yes, that's it, baby," Duncan urged. "Ride me, let it out!"

She did, rocking against him, scratching him, growling at him as if he were responsible for the pain tearing through her. She felt savage, unable to control herself. She raked at his chest, drawing blood as her nails tore through his skin. But he only smiled at her, his grin feral and filled with lust, his eyes glowing an eerie color.

"*Bruthainn, allaidh faoilleach*," he mumbled. She didn't understand the words, but she felt them touch her, deep inside her, like an explosion of fire bursting within her. "Hot," he whispered, digging his claws into her hips and thrusting into her. "Wild wolf. Fuck me, Harlee! Fuck me like the wolf you are," he commanded.

Yes, that's what it was. There was a wolf within her trying to get out. She had to let it out. It hurt. It hurt bad. Her blood burned and she was on fire.

Then Adrian climbed on behind her. He was touching her, kissing her back, her shoulder, her neck, rubbing her ass, rubbing something cold against her ass. She tried to buck him off, push him away, but he was too strong. She growled at him, tried to bite him, but he was too strong.

Then he spread her ass cheeks, still probing with something cold and sticky wet, something slick. He slid his finger there, inside her, inside her ass.

"Adrian, no," she said, growling at him.

"Yes, Harlee," he said, biting down on her shoulder.

Oh, God, she liked that. Liked him biting her. She felt the first tremors of orgasm and rocked against Duncan's cock, her juices spilling over his balls, felt him thrust against her and growl.

Adrian penetrated her ass with his finger, pushing past the tight muscle there. It burned. It felt good. Oh so good.

"I like it nasty. It burns. But I like it."

"I know you do, baby. You're a nasty little girl," Adrian said.

She felt like she was in a haze, that it wasn't even her talking, that the person inside her wasn't her anymore. But she liked this new person. Bold and free, wicked and wild, open to naughty and nasty things. She wanted to fuck. She wanted to fuck both of them.

"I want you in my ass, Adrian. Now!"

"Yeah, baby. I'm going to fuck that ass now. Bend forward."

She leaned over, far over, growling at Duncan as Adrian spread the cheeks of her buttocks apart. She bit Duncan's lip and he hissed at her, his eyes glowing hot red. She loved him like that, fucking his cock deep into her pussy and making her come hard. She was shaking so hard she couldn't see straight, and Adrian was probing with his cock head, searching that tight spot, pushing past the barrier.

She knew it was going to hurt, wanted it to hurt.

"Relax, Harlee, push back against me."

She did then cried out as he eased past the barrier and sheathed his cock in her ass.

She screamed and he was in her, pumping her, fucking her ass. God, it burned. She was on fire, her blood incinerating, her heart pumping so hard she knew she was going to explode.

A loud scream rent the air around them and she knew it was hers, a wailing cry she could not stop, nor could she stop the slamming orgasm that careened through her body. She was filled, utterly filled and transformed, no longer human, every organ and every part of her something new.

And these two men were part of her now, pumping her with their blood, their cum, their energy. Adrian leaned over her, driving his cock deep, filling her, tearing at her tight tissues as he drove harder, impaling her onto Duncan's shaft until she became one with them.

She was transformed now.

"I'm coming! Oh, God, I'm coming!" Again her climax crashed through her and she couldn't prevent it from taking control of her again. Her muscles squeezed pleasure from her, so exquisite it was painful. She bucked forward and back, and she didn't want to stop the sensations, only wanted to die from the pleasure of it as long as it kept on. And it did, until Adrian pulled out and away from her, releasing some of the intensity and she could breathe again. She collapsed against Duncan, feeling the rapid thrumming of his heart hammering against her palms, and didn't want to move.

But Adrian lifted her, despite her protests, carrying her upstairs and into the bathroom. He propped her up against the shower and turned it on, stepping in there with her and washing her body. She was too tired to move, just let him do everything, watching him soap her, rinse her, wash away the evidence of the men who had loved her, who had changed her.

"I really am different," she said, wonder invigorating her, inspiring her. Part of her had not believed it to be true.

"Yeah, you are. But we still don't know what part of you is dominant. That didn't come out yet."

She tilted her head. "So what does that mean?"

He shrugged. "Nothing." Reaching behind him, he shut the water off. "You're tired, let's get you dried off and into bed."

After she dried off, she walked into the bedroom. Duncan was there, freshly showered, no doubt from one of the other bathrooms. She looked to both men, realizing what she had to do.

"No, Harlee. You need to rest," Adrian warned.

"I have to know. We'll make it quick."

Duncan laughed. "As if that were possible."

"Make it hard. We can do this."

"No," Adrian insisted, but his cock was already lengthening.

She glared at him, at his shaft. "You want me again."

"Darlin', you'll be sore," Duncan said.

"Bullshit." She stepped to the oversized bed and threw back the cover, sliding underneath the cool sheets. "Fuck me. Both of you."

Chapter Thirteen

ഇ

She really did want to know. And God help her, her pussy pulsed with the need to feel them inside her again.

Shaking his head, Adrian slid in next to her on one side. She felt the weight of Duncan on her other side. She shivered and pressed her mouth to Adrian's lips, wrapping her hand around his cock, stroking his length, then reached for Duncan's, touching his thickness. She grew wet again as they hardened fully under her touch. Needing to see them both while she touched them, she shifted to her knees so she could watch their shafts as she stroked them with her hands.

She leaned in and captured Duncan's cock in her mouth, teasing the dark purple head with her tongue. Salty. She licked the pearly liquid off the tip, then turned to Adrian, swirling her tongue over the head and sucking his essence into her mouth, swallowing the dark flavor before moving back to Duncan and straddling him.

Placing her palms on his chest, she slid down the length of him, burying his cock in her pussy, keeping her eyes trained on Adrian as she rode Duncan hard. Adrian's nostrils flared as he watched her lifting up and down on Duncan's shaft. She leaned over and stroked Adrian, wondering what he was thinking. Did he enjoy watching Duncan's shaft disappearing into her cunt?

"Fuck him, baby," Adrian urged. "Feel it. Let it out."

Maybe Adrian was as turned on by all this as she was. She turned to Duncan then, watched his eyes glow, his face change, the hair thicken on his chest. The blood churned in her veins and she felt that strange power grow within her again. This time she concentrated on it, focused her energies within herself to try and draw it out. Pain centered in her bones, but along with the pain came a strength, a power she hadn't felt before. She felt stronger, more in control of it than before.

"That's it, darlin'," Duncan growled, his face changing shape, elongating, the angles sharpening. "Give it to me." His cock thickened inside her, stretching her inner walls until her juices poured onto his balls. She leaned back and howled as the bones in her fingers cracked, her nails turned into claws and she raked them along Duncan's thighs.

She'd never felt such power before and rocked against the thick cock inside her, feeling the orgasm approach like an oncoming wave. When it crashed, she screamed and held on, digging her claws into Duncan's chest, falling forward to bite at his mouth. He met her eagerly, growling into her open mouth, licking at her now-longer tongue. She was part human, part wolf now, her strength doubled, her orgasm incredible as wave after wave crashed over her.

She panted through the aftereffects of the amazing experience, her body moving back to fully human as quickly as she'd changed. Adrian pulled her off Duncan and threw her face down onto a pillow in the center of the bed, parted her legs and entered her from behind.

Wet and ready for him, she lifted her buttocks and met his thrust eagerly, her pussy still pulsing from her orgasm when he buried his cock inside her.

"Christ, you're so fucking wet."

He didn't even care that Duncan's cum was in her. She loved that about him, there were no recriminations about tonight, he said nothing about the fact that she'd just shifted into partial werewolf form. He wanted her, needed her, seemed desperate to have her.

"I need you, Adrian. I need you to fuck me. Hard."

"I know, baby." He shifted then plunged hard against her, his balls slapping her clit. Shards of exquisite pleasure quivered inside her, bringing her close to the brink yet again. She turned her head and saw that Duncan had left, but she couldn't think about where he'd gone. She curled her fingers into her palms and arched her back, raising her buttocks to give Adrian more of her.

"Harder, Adrian."

He thrust, with more force, at the same time swatting her buttocks with his palm. The sting made her flinch, but she raised her ass higher.

"More."

"You like to be spanked, don't you, Harlee?"

"Yes," she moaned, crying out when he swatted her again.

"Your cunt gets wetter when I spank you, Harlee. Did you know that?"

"More," she said, ignoring his question. She just needed to be fucked. Her blood burned. She was on fire again, needing something, a nameless, faceless force driving her on. She wanted pain. She was in pain, and nothing made sense other than what he gave her.

He smacked her again, harder this time. The sting helped and when he pulled back and pistoned his cock in deeper, she tilted her head back and screamed. Still, it wasn't enough.

"Adrian, please...help me!"

He leaned over, swept her hair to the side, and licked her neck. She heard the sizzle of her skin, then the stinging burn when he bit down on her flesh. Relief flooded her as he began to drink her life force, but then it got worse. She cried and tried to push him away, but he held firm to her neck as he continued to suck at her neck.

The orgasm slammed into her, freezing her to the spot as wave after wave of climactic rushing pleasure overcame her. She shuddered and screamed through it, tears flowing down her face. She'd never known pleasure like this, pain and ecstasy combined.

Adrian growled against her throat and filled her pussy with cum as he pumped deep in her. Again she felt that force within her, and Adrian flipped her over onto her back, staying connected to her, still pumping his cum into her. He released his bite on her neck and bared his throat to her.

"Take it, now!" he commanded.

Without thought, operating on instinct alone, she felt the long fangs drop down over her eyeteeth. A feral hunger flamed to life when she saw the beating pulse of his throat, a thirst she couldn't control. The need to feed was so overwhelming a tight knot formed in the pit of her stomach and she screamed.

"Feed, dammit!"

She closed her eyes and took what Adrian offered, her fangs slicing into the column of his throat, the coppery scent of his blood filling her nostrils as the hot taste of him burst into her mouth and she drank.

This. This was her ultimate power. Finally, her lust sated, she closed her eyes and knew she had found it, had found what she sought.

* * * * *

Eyes clenched tightly shut, Adrian was barely able to hold onto his strength as the orgasm continued to rocket through his body. He held on as Harlee's ferocious sucking took what little blood she knew how to take, as she merged with him in a way that shocked him even as he knew it completed them both.

She only drank for a few seconds before she released him, instinctively licked him to close the wound then promptly passed out. He dropped to the bed next to her, drawing her to him and curling his arm around her, totally dumbfounded at what had just happened.

Fucking hell! What just happened? He had not only mated with her, not only bitten her beyond just a passion bite, he had *claimed* her! Now what was he supposed to do about that?

A claiming wasn't something that could be hidden. It was a blood bond, a joining that went beyond the ritual. Without the sharing of a regular sexual bond they would both die. It was what kept mated vampires together.

Fuck! He inched out of her slumbering grasp and into the bathroom, turning on the cold shower, hoping the icy water would shock a little clarity into his sex-soaked mind.

She'd been wild. Hell, the entire night had been. He hadn't expected the magnitude of her sexual response to the ritual, hadn't been prepared for that. She'd turned into a wildcat, both demanding and responsive. Despite the arctic chill of the water, despite the number of times his sore dick had pummeled her, he was still getting hard recalling what they'd shared.

He shut off the water and stepped out, drying off and slipping on some clean clothes so he could find Duncan.

No doubt the vampire side of Harlee had revealed itself as dominant. Her need for blood had been more than her need to bond with Duncan. That much he could report to Robert. And he'd also have to tell him about the blood bond, unsure how Robert would react to the news since that hadn't been in the plan.

He found Duncan downstairs in the kitchen staring into a cup of steaming coffee. He poured a cup and sat next to him.

"She sleeping?" Duncan asked, not even looking up.

"Yeah."

He nodded and took a long swallow, seemingly content to sit there without talking. Adrian was fine with that too because at some point there were things he needed to explain to Duncan. Duncan had to be told what he had done to Harlee, how things had changed between them.

Now wasn't really a good time. First Adrian had to tell Robert.

First they all needed some damn sleep.

Adrian blew out a breath, about to suggest they all get a couple hours rest, when the guard at the front gate buzzed in. Adrian picked up and turned to Duncan.

"We've got visitors coming."

Duncan frowned but just then the front door flew open. They both pushed back their chairs and stood, tense and on instant alert. Sara flew into the room with a dozen of Robert's sentries trailing after her.

This couldn't be good. Her face was pale, her lips pressed together.

"What?" Adrian asked.

"Robert," she said, her lips trembling, her face tear streaked. "An attempt has been made on his life."

"What? How?"

"I'll explain in the helicopter. It's on the pad and still running. Get her. Let's go! He's near death and I don't know how much time we have. He has asked you to bring Harlee. Hurry!"

* * * * *

182

Harlee stared at the sleeping form of Robert, so pale and lifeless and looking so frail in the huge bed. So much had happened since last night, it still hadn't all registered in her mind.

This man who might die really was her uncle. These people gathered around the bed really were her family, and she really was a vampire.

Well, half vampire anyway. She couldn't begin to process everything that had happened with Duncan and Adrian. When Adrian had shaken her awake with news of Robert, that was all her mind could handle. She'd taken a quick shower and dressed, then sat mute in the helicopter, her hands clasped tightly together to still the trembling. They'd rushed right here and kept vigil over Robert and she'd prayed she wouldn't lose yet another member of a family she had yet to know.

Her heart ached, her stomach rolled and she fought back tears. She'd grown close to these people. They'd crept into her heart and become her family and she hadn't realized it. She didn't want to lose them. Any more of them, that is. She'd already lost her father, a man she hadn't even had the chance to know. She'd lost two parents she'd never had the chance to mourn.

She refused to lose any more family.

"How?" Adrian asked, turning to Sara.

"Some kind of blood poison. It was found in his donor drink last night."

Adrian frowned. "How could that happen? Blood is always thoroughly tested."

Sara shrugged and wrung her hands together. "I have no idea. It was just his glass too, and all the staff have been thoroughly questioned. Security is on it now. The lab is testing everything that came through the past twenty-four hours. We don't get to eat or drink anything that isn't thoroughly scanned first."

Harlee watched the play of emotions on Adrian's face. She knew he blamed himself for not being here. But why? He couldn't have done anything to prevent this from happening. She wanted to go to him, wrap her arms around him and offer him comfort but sensed he wouldn't welcome it right now.

"Harlee."

The sound of a strained whisper and the weak squeeze of her hand startled her. She turned her head to Robert, her heart pounding when she saw his eyes open.

"You're awake!"

She started to move out of the way so the doctor could examine him, but he held onto her hand. "He can wait. I'm fine, feeling stronger already."

"Really, Robert, it's necessary—" the doctor started, nearly jerking Harlee from the chair. She hurried out of it to give him access to her uncle.

"I said I'm fine!"

The strength, the commanding tone, was already returning to his voice. Harlee exhaled a sigh of relief. The doctor hurriedly backed away and nodded and Harlee resumed her seat next to his bed, sliding her hand in his. "Obviously everyone sees you're feeling just fine," she said with a wink. "I'm glad."

"And you seem fine yourself," he said. "I trust you had a fruitful evening?"

"I have a lot to talk to you about," she said, keeping her voice a whisper. "There's plenty of time to talk when you're feeling better. I'd really like you to rest now."

He nodded. "Spoken like a true member of our clan. On that, I will sleep well." He drew her hand up to his mouth and kissed the back of it, then looked to Duncan and Adrian. "Guard her well. Someone wants us all dead."

Adrian and Duncan both nodded.

"We'll need to get out so he can rest," she said, for some reason feeling empowered to take charge. She nodded at the doctor as she passed by, ignoring the wide-eyed stares of those in the room.

Adrian just smirked at her and followed her out the door.

She, Duncan and Adrian assembled in the living room, where she felt it was time they had a serious conversation about what occurred last night. She had to talk to both of them about her feelings, about her dominant side and what it meant for both their nations. And they had to figure out who was trying to systematically eliminate the leaders of the vampire and lycan clans.

"Something's been bugging me since that day we were attacked in the SUV," Duncan said when they entered the small room and shut the door.

"What?" Adrian asked.

"I was hit with a silver-laced bullet. Understandable since we left from the lycan mansion. If it was government assassins and they had made the house as a lycan location, it would stand to reason they would use ammo to take down werewolves. But they also used the laser light grenades and were shooting UV laser fire, which meant they were also targeting vampires."

Adrian sat back and stared at Duncan. "I hadn't considered that with everything that had been going on, but you're right. Why the hell were they firing both?"

"Unless they weren't from the government," Harlee finished for them. "I have something I need to tell both of you and you aren't going to like it."

"What is it?" Adrian asked.

She blurted it out before she lost her nerve. "I work for the government. I worked...for the government, as a psychologist. Interrogating lycans and vampires, trying to learn about them, about their minds, so the government could use what I could find out about them...use what I could find out against them."

They stared at her as if she'd just sprouted horns and claimed to be the child of Beelzebub.

"You work against us?" Duncan asked.

"No!" She stood and wrapped her arms around her middle. "I mean yes. I mean I used to. I didn't know! About you, about Adrian, about any of this! I didn't know about you, about us. How could I? The government told us that lycans and vampires were vicious, savage creatures out to take over, to kill all humans. We didn't know otherwise, how could we? I only knew what I was told."

God, please believe me. She prayed they understood. But they just stared at her as if they contemplated whether to trust her or not. "When you first brought me here, I thought you knew I worked for the government. I thought I was being kidnapped. When Robert told me I was Stefan and Amelia's daughter, I thought it was bullshit. I wasn't raised as a vampire or lycan, I was raised human. I didn't know any differently. I was raised to think that vampires and werewolves were my enemy, not my family.

"And now?" Adrian asked, his brow arched.

She knew what he wanted to hear. Now she had to hope he believed what she was about to tell him came from her heart. "Now I'm part of all of you, all of this," she whispered, tears filling her eyes.

Don't make me leave. Not when I just found you. Not when I love you.

She waited what seemed like an eternity while they both looked at her, deciding her fate. Her stomach rolled, pain coursing through her. What if they made her leave, or something even worse?

"Tell us everything you know," Adrian said, sitting down and pointing to the couch. "Now that you're one of us, your inside information can help us free the hostages."

She hadn't realized she'd held her breath so long until she finally expelled it, her legs so weak she fell onto the couch next to him.

Finally, she felt like she belonged.

Harlee told them where she worked, her security clearance, everything she'd done and found out about the lycans and vampires that were being held at the government location.

"They're fine. They're fed and taken care of. As far as I know, they haven't been harmed, but my clearance isn't that high. All I do is talk to them. I'm not privy to a lot of the experimentation that's being done on them."

But she was guilty by association. The government had held them against their will for years, trying to find out the whereabouts of the lycan and vampire nation headquarters by hypnosis and by drugging them and by God only knows what other methods she knew nothing about.

"But as far as you know they hadn't revealed anything," Adrian said.

She shook her head, feeling miserable that she had taken part in these experiments. How could she have known, though? Still, why didn't she feel the part of her that was lycan and vampire? Why didn't that part of her prevent her from persecuting her own people? She felt miserable inside. Miserable and guilty.

"Okay," Adrian said, standing and pacing. "This is what we have to do first."

Duncan's cell phone rang and he pulled it to his ear, then shut it just as quickly and turned to them. "An attempt has been made on William's life. Silver bullet. Lester's frantic. I've got to go." He looked to Harlee and then back at Adrian.

"Go. I'll grab Sara and Annmarie. We'll guard Harlee."

Duncan nodded and hurried from the room.

"Shit. This isn't good. Something is going on and it's happening all at once. This is a concentrated effort to take down all the higher-ups in the lycan and vampire organization. Come with me," Adrian said, holding out his hand to Harlee and leading her from the room.

Chapter Fourteen

ॐ

William was only slightly injured, the silver bullet grazing his ribs, but not penetrating. Already closing, the wound had left him weak, but fortunately not enough silver had penetrated his bloodstream to kill him. He was resting but would recover.

Duncan sat in the lycan offices with Lester, more irritated than worried. Things just didn't add up.

Why hadn't an attempt been made on Lester's life? Why William instead?

Unless Lester wasn't made a target because Lester was involved in planning the systematic assassinations. And maybe William wasn't dead because Lester didn't have the guts to go through with it and kill his own son but wanted to take the suspicion off himself by making the attempt on William's life.

Lester sat behind his desk, looking pale, grief-stricken and anxious.

"I really would like to return to my son's bedside if you don't mind, Duncan," Lester said, tapping his fingers on the desktop.

"In a minute," Duncan said, trying to get his thoughts straight. "Tell me again where you were when William was attacked."

"Right here in my study, as I told you earlier."

"And who else was here?"

"No one."

"How convenient."

Lester's eyes narrowed. "Just what are you implying, Duncan? That I would harm my own son? For what possible purpose?"

"You tell me." None of this made sense, but the options were narrowing and Duncan couldn't rely on what made sense any longer. He had to look at all the possible suspects. With Robert and William and Harlee out of the picture, Lester would control all of the holdings of Dark Moon. He didn't want to look at Lester as a suspect, but he had to start somewhere and Lester was the highest on the list.

"I love my son, Duncan. You of all people should know that." Lester stood and walked to the window, staring out at the full moon above. "I loved my brother as well. I will mourn his death until the day I die. Investigate anything you like about me. My life is an open book and I won't stand in your way." He turned to Duncan, genuine grief evident in his eyes. "I have nothing to hide."

Duncan nodded and rose from the chair. "I need to head back to the vampire mansion. You going to be okay?"

Lester nodded. "I ordered extra security all around the perimeter and on both myself and William. You can put your own top people on me if it makes you feel better. The people you trust the most. Do whatever makes you comfortable. I understand your investigation is for the good of our people, Duncan. I don't fault you for that."

He saw the sincerity in Lester's eyes and nodded, still not sure whether to believe him or not.

Duncan left and took the elevator to the basement parking garage, lifting his keys and punching the button to disarm the alarm on his SUV. He reached for the door handle when something sharp struck the back of his head. A sticky wetness rolled down his neck and his knees began to buckle.

Fuck! He'd been had. How stupid.

Then all he saw was blackness.

* * * * *

Harlee paced her room, hating being confined and watched like a caged animal.

"Are you sure the lycan side of you isn't dominant?" Annmarie teased. "I think you're about to growl at all of us."

Harlee stuck her tongue out at her.

Annmarie laughed. "I'm sure you meant to point that weapon at Adrian, honey, not me."

Annmarie fell back onto Harlee's bed and stretched, the diamond jewel in her belly button like a multicolored prism under the overhead lights.

"This is boring," Annmarie said.

"You could try knitting," Adrian said, leaning against the wall and crossing his arms.

Sara snorted.

"Fuck off," Annmarie replied with a bored yawn. "That's more Sara's pastime since she can't get laid these days."

"You're such a whore, Annmarie," Sara said, shaking her head.

Annmarie leaned up on her elbows and grinned. "Why thank you, Sara."

Harlee rolled her eyes but couldn't suppress her grin. "How long are we going to have to hole up here, anyway?"

"I'm waiting to hear from Duncan," Adrian said. "In fact, he should have been back here by now." He pulled out his cell phone and dialed, then frowned, then dialed again. "Nothing. Odd." He dialed again then frowned again.

"What's wrong?" she asked.

"Duncan's not answering his cell phone."

"Maybe he's somewhere where he's not getting a signal."

"There's nowhere out of reach between here and there. I don't like this. I'm going to try the lycan mansion."

He dialed and spoke to someone for a few seconds, then hung up and cursed.

"The guard said Duncan left over an hour and a half ago and said he was headed right back here. This isn't good. He should have been back by now, or called. And he wouldn't have gone anywhere else. Something's wrong."

"Go," Sara said to Adrian. "I know you want to look for him or figure out what's happened. Annmarie and I can stay here and guard Harlee. Go on. She'll be fine."

"Sara's right, much as I hate to agree with her," Annmarie said. "Go find Duncan."

Adrian nodded. "You'll be okay?" he asked Harlee.

She rolled her eyes and opened the door. "There are a billion guards roaming the halls. An army couldn't get to me. Go find him. I'm worried."

He left and she closed the door, sitting on the bed with Sara and Annmarie, feeling like a stupid, helpless female.

"Well, this sucks," Harlee said. "Why is it the men are all out figuring out who the assassins are and the women are wringing their hands while locked up in the bedroom?"

"Good question," Annmarie said with a wry smile. "We're just as strong and capable as they are. We should be able to work this out in our heads. Besides, we have the pussy. That gives us extra brain cells."

Harlee laughed out loud.

"Now, ladies," Sara said, holding up her hands. "Something must have happened to Duncan. And Adrian is just making calls. Let's just do what they asked us to do."

"Oh go knit something, you dimwit," Annmarie said, then turned to Harlee. "Okay, so what have we got here? Let's piece it together from the beginning."

"I'm going to check on Robert," Sara sniffed, storming out the door in a huff.

"I thought she'd never leave," Annmarie said.

Harlee giggled.

They spent the better part of an hour going over everything that had happened from the time Stefan was killed until Duncan failed to show up. They ended up ruling out the human government, deciding it had to be an inside job, but they couldn't determine whether it was inside the lycan or vampire house.

"It could be a combination of both," Harlee suggested.

Annmarie wrinkled her nose. "I find it hard to believe that any vampire or lycan would join forces like that. It's not unheard of, but we just don't…mingle that well, if you know what I mean. Or at least we haven't before."

"But control of both organizations is a very big lure. Putting differences aside for a prize like that might be worth it," Harlee suggested.

Annmarie shrugged. "Good point."

But who would want to do that? She didn't know enough of them to even make the suggestion and that was more frustrating than anything.

"So, you're in love with my cousin."

Harlee's eyes widened at the abrupt turn in subject but she nodded. "Big time."

Annmarie shook her head. "You are so fucked."

Harlee laughed.

"Have you told him yet?"

"I haven't had time with all this going on."

193

"And how does he feel about everything?"

"I don't know. It was all so wild last night. And the biting and the drinking of blood. Wow."

Annmarie arched a brow. "Who drank whose blood?"

"Both of us. Why?"

"No reason," she said, smiling. "Interesting."

"You know something. Tell me."

"Not my place to tell. Really, really interesting. Who'd have thought it?"

"Thought what?" Now Annmarie had her curious. She knew something. Something about the dual biting. "What about the biting, Annmarie?"

Annmarie was about to speak but they were interrupted by a shrill alarm. The sounds of shouting had them both starting and flying off the bed toward the door. Annmarie put out her hand and shouted, "Stay here! I'm going to see what's going on! Lock the door behind me and don't let anyone in but me, Adrian or Sara, okay?"

Harlee nodded and did as Annmarie asked, bolting the door behind her, then began counting the minutes. If somebody didn't come back here shortly, she was going out there to see what the hell was going on. She wasn't helpless. She was a trained agent. Put a goddamned gun in her hand and she could take care of herself. She could fire a weapon.

She could help, dammit! She reached for the door handle, scared shitless when she heard a knock. She jumped then said, "Who is it?"

"Sara!"

Breathing out a sigh of relief, she unlocked the door and opened it. Sara slipped in and closed the door behind her, locking it.

"What's going on?" Harlee asked.

"Someone breached the security perimeter. All hell is breaking loose around here. I've been instructed to take you to a safer location. We're locking everything down."

"This is crazy," Harlee said, running her fingers through her hair.

"I know," Sara said, motioning for Harlee to follow her.

She headed to the far wall and Harlee frowned but followed anyway. Sara pulled the corner of a picture askew and a panel in the wall moved.

"Well, that's cool."

"Always helpful to have an escape plan," Sara said with a grin, flipping a switch and illuminating a narrow set of stairs.

A musty smell greeted her as she entered the stairwell. The steps were concrete and her voice echoed as she spoke. "What about Adrian and Annmarie?"

"Adrian is seeing to security and Annmarie is with Robert. They're meeting us down here shortly. Robert is fine and he's well guarded."

"Good." Prickles of sensation caused the hairs to stand up on the back of her neck. Something wasn't right but she couldn't put her finger on what it was. She suddenly felt like going down here was wrong.

"Sara," she said, suddenly stopping.

Sara looked up at her, concern on her frowning face. "What's wrong?"

"I don't know. Something. Just a weird sensation."

"That's just your new power. You'll get used to it. You're sensing danger and rightly so. We need to hurry." She turned away and kept moving.

Harlee stood there for a few more seconds, debating whether to head back upstairs or follow Sara. If she went back upstairs, she knew what would happen. She'd run into Adrian who'd call her ten different idiots for not following orders.

Shit. She hated being new at this and not knowing what to do. Why didn't being a vampire come with some kind of instruction manual? At least when she was a human what she was supposed to do and not do was written down in black and white. Now she had to operate on instinct, and she didn't know if her instincts were right or wrong right now.

She followed Sara, hoping she hadn't fucked up and made the wrong choice.

They reached the bottom of the stairs and Sara pulled out keys and approached a thick, ancient door that looked to be made out of solid oak.

"How long has this been here?"

"Too long for me to even remember. The newer part of Dark Moon was built over what had stood for centuries, pre-dating most of our existence. This was a hideaway for the early vampires who had settled here from Europe." She slipped the huge key in and turned the lock, then yanked on the door. Dust flew out at them and Harlee choked, helping Sara pull back the six-inch thick door. Sara reached in on the floor and felt around, pulling up a lantern and used a match to light it, then led Harlee into a small room filled only with an old oak table and matching set of chairs. Along the wall were old shackles midway and on the floor.

"Looks like an old torture chamber or something," Harlee remarked.

"No kidding," Sara said. "I've never been down here." Sara inspected the iron shackles, wrapping one around her wrist. "Get a load of these things. They're heavy!"

Sara handed off the lantern to Harlee, who lifted it toward the shackles. She let Sara wrap one around her, feeling its weight. "Wow, they are heavy."

Harlee winced when she heard the click of the shackle, knowing instantly she'd been had. Sara wrenched the lantern from Harlee's grasp, slammed Harlee's hand against the wall and fixed the second shackle around her other wrist.

Pain shot up Harlee's arm as she fought, but Sara was strong and Harlee was nearly doubled over in agony. Fuck! How stupid could she be?

When Sara lit the other lanterns in the room, she didn't need to see the light shining on Sara's face to know what she'd see there.

Pure, venomous hatred.

"Too easy," Sara said, satisfaction on her smiling face. "Such a child, such trusting innocence. You played right into my hand."

"I can't believe you tried to kill your own brother!" Harlee spat, kicking Sara's shins. She knew she couldn't hurt her, nevertheless it gave her some comfort to cause her a minimal amount of discomfort.

Sara's eyes narrowed and she stepped back. "You couldn't possibly hurt me in any way, little girl, so don't even try. And my brother, along with a lot of other people, stand in the way of what I want most."

"What's that? Power?"

"Of course. Power is the most attractive thing. With power I can have anything I want."

Sara's eyes had begun to shine in that way Harlee had seen in her patients all too often over the years, when madness took over and sanity disappeared. She had hidden it very well.

"You might think you can have everything you want, honey, but you'll never have Adrian." Harlee knew it was a cheap shot, but it was the only weapon she had. And keeping Sara off balance could work to her advantage.

Sara whirled and clutched her by the throat, her fangs emerging. "I can have anything, *anything* I want, including the man I want, you bitch!" she hissed. She pulled back and slapped Harlee across the face so hard her lip split. Harlee tasted blood and her eye began to swell shut, but she refused to wince in front of the deranged woman.

"He's mine, Sara. I love him and he loves me, and nothing you do can change that, no power you wield will make him yours." Though Harlee didn't know that to be the case, Sara didn't know that.

"Not true. Once you're dead he will want me. You won't matter to him."

"I will always matter to him. I'm his mate now." That's what Annmarie had intimated at. She might not have a vampire owner's manual, but she could at least put two and two together in that respect.

"You are not!" Sara's eyes widened and she came at Harlee with a gun drawn, swinging it at Harlee. Harlee kicked at Sara's arm and the weapon went off as it hit Sara. A burning fire rushed through Harlee's leg. Harlee gasped but didn't cry out.

"You did *not* mate with him!" Sara cried. "Tell me you did not mate with him!"

Harlee's fangs slid down and she hissed at Sara, fighting the chains that bound her. "Of course I mated with him," Harlee spat out, wanting to hurt Sara, lashing out at the woman and wanting to feed the madness she saw there. If she could keep Sara off kilter, maybe there was a way to escape. "He doesn't want you, Sara. He wants me."

"I knew the vampire side of you would be dominant! I knew it! One more person to stand in my way! First Robert favored Amelia, and then you had to come along, making yet another person I needed to get rid of!" Sara stormed back and forth, muttering to herself as if Harlee wasn't even there.

Harlee stared down at the blood pouring down her leg, hoping she didn't bleed to death, hoping to hell someone figured out where she was before this lunatic bitch killed her.

"Honey, it doesn't matter if you kill me. You will never make it to the top. You are too fucking nuts."

"No!" Sara said, turning on her again. "I will rule the vampire nation! You will die!"

"Why are you believing the little bitch's lies, Sara? She's just upsetting you."

Sara turned at the sound of a male voice. "She is lying, isn't she, William? Tell me she's lying."

Now it all made perfect sense. William. The other half of the puzzle.

He stood in the doorway looking perfectly healthy.

"Of course," Harlee said. "William took care of the killings on the lycan side, and you on the vampire side. It would take both of you to pull this off, and you both had something to gain."

"See, Sara, I warned you she wasn't as dumb as she looked," William said, stepping up to her to lick the blood from the side of her lip. Harlee wrenched away, revulsion turning her stomach, but William held her face in a vise-like grip.

"Get your disgusting hands off me," Harlee said, allowing the lycan within her to free itself, mixing it with the vampire to increase her strength. She pulled at the chains, feeling her power double her strength, stopping the blood flow of the wound in her leg and breaking the chains holding her. She growled at William and pushed him backward. His eyes widened and he fell to the ground.

She couldn't beat both of them, but she could maybe take down one of them. Her power might be new and raw, but she had some at least. She kicked at William while he was on the floor, mindful of Sara scrambling for her weapon. Leveling a blow at William's face with her foot, she heard the satisfied crunch of his nose breaking under her booted heel and his resulting howling cry.

She took off after Sara, launching herself at the woman just as Sara reached her gun. Landing on Sara's thighs, she used all her strength to wrestle the gun from Sara's grasp, then did the only thing she knew how to do. She held onto Sara's wrists and bit down on the woman's throat. The lycan and vampire mingled within her, and she tore the woman's throat open. In seconds Sara lay limp beneath her and Harlee stood, blood dripping from her mouth. She wiped it away with the back of her hand, feeling no remorse for what she had done.

Panting for breath, she turned to find William, his face swollen and bloody, pointing a gun at her.

"You're dead, bitch." His face began to change and he grew taller, broader, the lycan within him bursting forth. She knew she didn't have half the power and strength he had.

At least she managed to get one of them. Too tired to fight anymore, she closed her eyes and awaited her impending death with resolve, but just then something brushed by her and her eyes flew open. William screamed as Duncan in partial wolf form flew through the air, a loud piercing howl resounding through the room. In an instant, William lay sprawled on the floor, dead, his throat torn away, much as she'd done to Sara.

Her strength gone, she crumpled to the floor, fighting for breath.

From behind her, Adrian rushed to her side and picked her up, cradling her against his chest. "It's over, baby, you're all right."

Duncan shifted and stood over William, looking at Harlee with concern.

"I'm okay," she said. "Thank you. Are you all right?"

"Bastard conked me on the head but I'm fine," Duncan said. "Can't believe the sonofabitch managed to pull one over on me. Glad I had a chance to rip his fucking throat out."

"Me too," she said, then looked up at Adrian and smiled, but that's all she could manage as the pain and weakness took over.

Shit. She hated weakness. Didn't the vampire owner's manual say something about not being weak anymore?

She closed her eyes and passed out.

Chapter Fifteen

ॐ

Harlee woke and stretched, realizing the sun streaming in through the windows of her bedroom was becoming a bit bothersome. Okay, so being a vampire meant her sun-worshiping days were over. She squinted and rolled out of the bed, shielding her eyes while she walked over to the window and shut the blinds.

"That's better," she mumbled, realizing that her leg was already healed. She looked down and saw a tiny pink spot where yesterday a big gaping hole stood. "This lycan and vampire thing is pretty darn cool."

And she was talking to herself. That was new too.

"You're talking to yourself. And I guess I should stop walking in on you while you're naked. Too bad. I'll miss that.

She whirled at the sound of Duncan's voice and grinned. "Why? Is seeing me naked something you're not used to by now?

His brow shot up and he looked her over from head to toe, advancing on her with a stealth-like grace she'd grown to admire.

"I could never grow tired of admiring a body like yours." He stopped in front of her and laced his fingers around her waist, drawing her close and pressing a kiss to her lips that made her sigh. When he drew back, she saw a brief flicker of regret in his eyes. "But that gorgeous body doesn't belong to me and it never did."

Now it was her turn to arch a brow. "Really. And just who does my body belong to?"

"As if you didn't know. Your dominant power is vampire, darlin'. And your love for Adrian is evident. I saw it the night we all joined. It was obvious."

"I see." Nothing like being told who she belonged to. She wasn't sure if she liked that or not. She wasn't somebody's possession, and she didn't like being ping-ponged between the two of them as if she didn't get to choose.

Not that she hadn't chosen. Or rather her heart had chosen. Whatever.

"Everything wrapped up?" she asked, deciding to ignore the subject of her heart.

"Yeah. Lester is a basket case. Apologizing to everyone for William's part in all of this, horrified that his son killed Stefan and was involved in trying to kill Robert. He had no idea of the lengths to which William and Sara would go to control the lycan and vampire nations. Hell, none of us had any clue. Robert had no clue how delusional Sara had become. We all knew she had a bit of a screw loose, but not that much. And we knew William was ambitious, but not that he planned to pin all the assassinations on his own father."

Harlee shook her head. "I've seen it before. The lengths people will go to for power. It's a very heady lure."

"Power makes people insane. Or at least corrupt. Me, I just like sex. And speaking of sex," he said, wagging his eyebrows at her.

She laughed. "You have a one-track mind and I'm trying to change the subject, Duncan."

"Harlee, you're a beautiful, special woman. But you're not *my* woman. And you do love Adrian. You can deny it all you want, but the love is there in your eyes."

"That I do," she admitted.

"But?"

Should she admit her uncertainties? "I don't know about Adrian."

"You mean you don't know how he feels about you."

"Yes."

"Easy enough to find out. He's on his way up here."

Her eyes widened. "He is? Oh shit!" She scanned the room for her robe, spotting it on the chair and heading for it. Duncan grabbed her wrist.

"Uh-uh. You want to know how he feels about you? Let's find out right now."

"No, Duncan!"

She tried to jerk from his grasp, but he tipped her chin and wrapped her in a tight clinch, kissing her just as the door opened. Without looking, Harlee knew it was Adrian. The musky scent of him filled her from across the room, aphrodisiac to her senses.

Duncan lifted his lips from hers, his sea-blue eyes filled with teasing mirth.

Uh-oh.

"You're a special man, Duncan," she whispered. "Warped, but special. Somewhere out there is one special woman for you."

"God, I hope not," he whispered back, holding her tight. "What fun would that be?"

Adrian coughed. Duncan pulled away and winked at her. Harlee reached for her robe and slipped it on, catching Adrian's scowl as he entered the room.

This was going to be interesting. She almost felt guilty for leading him on this way.

Almost.

"Was I interrupting?" he asked.

"No," Duncan said. "We had just finished." He made a show of adjusting his zipper.

Harlee stifled a laugh and Duncan caught and held her hand. "The other night with the three of us was somethin', darlin'. I think we should do it regularly, don't you? A regular threesome?"

"You think so?" she replied, slipping into the chair and grabbing the pot of coffee sitting there to pour a cup.

"Are you two out of your fucking minds?" Adrian said.

"Why?" Duncan asked, slipping into the other chair and filling a cup. "Any reason you wouldn't want to do that? Can't say I had anything to complain about, Adrian. Surely you didn't either, from the way you fucked her."

"Enough, Duncan," he warned, glaring.

"Nah, I can't say I had nearly enough of Harlee's pussy the other night. Not nearly enough. I say we go at it again tonight."

"That's it!" Adrian advanced on him and Duncan shot out of the chair like a bullet. The two of them were nose to nose in an instant and Harlee just stared at both of them in shock. Adrian's face was red with rage, Duncan's lips curled in amusement.

"So, Harlee, I guess you have your answer. I think I need to go now." He backed away from Adrian, picked up Harlee's hand and kissed it, and sauntered from the room.

Harlee grinned at his departure, then turned to Adrian, hands on hips. "Well?"

"Well what?"

Oh, he was really pissed. His face was contorted in rage and his fangs exposed. "What was that all about?" she asked, keeping her voice calm and even despite the tension emanating from him.

"What?"

"That macho display of temper. You have something to say, then say it."

"Fine." He turned away from the door where Duncan had retreated and faced her. "The other night when I bit you, the bite was a little more…permanent, because that time when I bit you, you bit me. Which means we mated. A blood bond. It's like a vampire marriage."

"And this means?"

"It means there will be no more ménages. You don't get to fuck anyone else. I don't get to fuck anyone else."

"You were going to tell me this when?"

"I was going to get around to it, dammit. I've been busy." He glared at her as if this was all somehow her fault.

Harlee rolled her eyes. "Gee, that was romantic." She turned away, sat back in the chair and picked up her coffee.

"That's it? That's all you have to say?"

"Yes." She sipped her coffee and reached for the newspaper.

"Goddamit, Harlee!" He stormed over, threw the paper on the floor, tossed the coffee cup across the room and hauled her to her feet, pinning her arms at her sides. "You have to goddamned pay attention while I'm trying to tell you I love you."

Her eyes widened. "That was an *I love you*?"

"It is now. I love you. I'm not very good at this sort of thing."

"Clearly." Her lips twitched, warmth flooding her body. "I love you too, Adrian. Now kiss me."

He did, his mouth descending on hers, first rough, as if he were angry that he loved her. But then his lips gentled and his arms came around her back, his body molding to hers. He cradled her head in the back of his hand, the other resting on the small of her back.

It was perfect. It was romantic, the way love was supposed to be. Just the two of them and he was holding her, and her heart was pounding against his, her blood boiling with need for him. Her pussy throbbed and moistened and she rocked it against his hard-on, whimpering against his mouth.

He tore his lips away and stared at her, his eyes dark as he pulled the robe from her shoulders and pushed her back against the wall. Time stood still as they stared into each other's eyes while he unzipped his jeans and pulled out his cock.

Harlee reached for his shaft, felt the throbbing pulse of his life force and stroked it, rewarded with a drop of pre-cum gathering at the slit. She rubbed her thumb over his cock head and he groaned. She shuddered at the sound, bringing her thumb to her mouth to taste his salty fluid. He took her mouth and sucked his own juices off her tongue, sucking harder while he positioned his cock between her folds and lifted her leg over his hip, then thrust inside her.

She cried out, her blood on fire, her fangs descending and biting into his lip as he fucked her. Tiny quakes of pleasure pulsed in her pussy with every thrust of his cock, drawing her closer and closer to the precipice of completion. He groaned and his canines descended, pricking her lower lip and drawing blood. They drank of each other as they made love, drawing their strength with each thrust and suck of their tongues. Harlee tightened against him and cried out, flooding him with her juices as she came, shuddering.

Adrian groaned against her mouth and bit hard on her lip, pouring his cum into her pussy as she held tight to him and closed her eyes, wanting it to go on forever.

When it was over, she retracted her fangs, licking his wounds until they closed, feeling more complete, more satisfied than she ever had before. She wanted to hold onto him like this forever, never let him go. He swept her into his arms and carried her to the bed, climbing in next to her and pulling the covers over them both.

She liked feeling his chest against her back, his arm over her, cupping her breast, the rhythmic beating of his heart against her. With Adrian at her side, she felt safe, complete.

But she also knew there were loose ends that needed to be tied up, things left undone.

"The government is going to wonder where I am."

"I know. But you are the 'in' to help free our people. We'll work it out."

Somehow she knew that. And for the first time in a very long time, she felt she had a purpose. Maybe the first time ever. She hadn't realized until just this moment that maybe she'd never felt…needed. And now she did. Her "family" needed her. Both her families—the vampires and the lycans.

"I love you, Harlee. I've never said that to a woman before."

Somehow she knew that too. "I love you too, Adrian."

The rest would fall into place. This was only the beginning.

About Jaci Burton

ɛͻ

In April 2003, Ellora's Cave foolishly offered me a contract for my first erotic romance and I haven't shut up since. My writing is an addiction for which there is no cure, a disease in which strange characters live in my mind, all clamoring for their own story. I try to let them out one by one, as mixing snarling werewolves with a bondage and discipline master can be very dangerous territory. Then again, unusual plotlines offer relief from the demons plaguing me.

In my world, well-endowed, naked cabana boys do the vacuuming and dishes, little faeries flit about dusting the furniture and doing laundry, Wolfgang Puck fixes my dinner and I spend every night engaged in wild sexual abandon with a hunky alpha. Okay, the hunky alpha part is my real life husband and he keeps my fantasy life enriched with extensive "research". But Wolfgang won't answer my calls, the faeries are on strike and my readers keep running off with the cabana boys.

About C. J. Burton

ɛͻ

CJ Burton lives in Oklahoma with his author wife Jaci, daughter, three dogs and a beta fish. He has done first edits and provided help with male dialogue and point-of- view for Jaci since she started writing. Somehow or another this resulted in Jaci and many of her readers badgering him into co-writing a book with her. When he has time he enjoys golfing, weight lifting, playing computer games and just hanging out with Jaci and his daughter.

Jaci and CJ welcomes comments from readers. You can find her website and email address on her author bio page at www.ellorascave.com

*A*lso by Jaci Burton

ಌ

Enjoy an excerpt from:
ANIMAL INSTINCTS

Copyright © JACI BURTON, 2005.

All Rights Reserved, Ellora's Cave, Inc.

Animal Instincts

Dressed entirely in black PVC leather, she strutted every inch of her goddess-like body in stiletto thigh-high boots, her silvery-blonde ponytail swinging from side to side as she approached. Full breasts swelled and threatened to spill over the top of the corset.

The closer she got, the more pronounced her frown became. Did she recognize him? Did she sense the same thing he did? Or was she really as clueless about what was inside her as he thought? If she knew, she'd have sought him out, he was sure of it.

The only reason he came here was because he didn't want to approach her at the clinic, and didn't want to scare the shit out of her by showing up at her apartment. He'd been watching her for weeks now, ever since he first picked up her scent at the clinic and realized there was more to Moonlight Madison than he'd ever guessed. And every time he saw her, he became more convinced she didn't have a clue about him, or about herself.

She stopped in front of him, her head tilted slightly as she scanned his body from head to toe.

The movement exposed her neck, one of his favorite parts on a woman. So tender, so sensitive, it aroused him just thinking about possessing that slender column of flesh, burying his teeth in her nape and holding onto her as he fucked her. The creamy expanse of her throat would look nice with a collar around it, too. As long as he held the leash.

He inhaled her sweet scent, thankful she hadn't tried to mask it with one of those cloying perfumes women sometimes wore.

"You're Blake Hunter. From the clinic."

He wasn't sure she'd acknowledge that she knew him. "Yeah."

"Figures," she mumbled low enough that the average person wouldn't hear. Then again, he wasn't an average person.

He also wondered what she meant. She looked disappointed. As many times as he'd been to the clinic to pick up medicine for the refuge, he'd never spoken directly to her. She was always in the background doing something and his dealings had usually been with the receptionist or the doc. But he'd seen her. Knew she volunteered there and went to vet school part-time.

He still couldn't get over the transformation. Her typical worn blue jeans and an oversized T-shirt were night and day different from the sex bombshell getup she wore now.

Not that he minded her current attire. Either way, she excited him. A helluva lot as a matter of fact. He itched to throw her down on the floor of the lobby and shove his hard cock inside her, sink his teeth into the soft flesh of her shoulder and hold her in place while he rode her to a hard climax. He shuddered and pushed the beast away.

Not yet.

She moved to the reception counter and rested her elbow on the dark wood, looking perfectly calm and in control. The image she presented was a woman used to taking charge. At least externally.

Her brow lifted as she picked up the paper, scanned it and shot him a questioning look.

Yeah, he'd paid for her for the entire night. One hour wouldn't do it. He'd need the whole night and more with her. Then, if everything went as he hoped, they'd have an eternity together.

"Are you sure about this?" she asked, waving the receipt at him as she left the desk.

"Yeah."

"It's a lot of money."

"I *have* a lot of money. Let's get started."

Shrugging, she motioned him toward the hallway. "It's your dime. Follow me."

Blake sucked in a deep breath and tried to keep from drooling as he followed her fine ass down the dimly lit corridor. The corset thing and tight little panties she wore fit high over her curvy hips and narrowed across her buttocks, showing more than a little of her shapely ass.

His cock saluted its appreciation of her body. He didn't like overly skinny women. She had a woman's body. A real woman's body. Tits, ass, hips, legs that went on forever and thighs made for a man to ride between. Yeah, she was built perfectly in all the right places.

Places he'd like to lick, suck, bite and fuck. And he would. All in good time.

First he had to figure out how much she knew. If she hadn't realized anything yet, he'd just have to give her a little nudge in the right direction, because the moon was full, the beast within him was clawing to get out, and he wasn't going to wait one more goddamned minute to have her.

She might be the dominatrix in this place, she might cater to the kind of men who begged to be told what to do by a woman, but he was no more that kind of man than he was fully human.

As she led him back to what he assumed was her room, he smiled at the confident sway of her hips. Yeah, she thought she was in charge here, but he was about to turn the tables on her. Soon he'd have her cuffed, naked and pleading with him to fuck her.

His balls ached just thinking about giving her exactly what he knew she wanted, what she needed, what she craved. He knew enough about her to know that the lifestyle she led wasn't fulfilling her. Hell, he knew more about her needs than she did.

Something was missing in Moonlight Madison's life.

Him.

Why an electronic book?

We live in the Information Age—an exciting time in the history of human civilization in which technology rules supreme and continues to progress in leaps and bounds every minute of every hour of every day. For a multitude of reasons, more and more avid literary fans are opting to purchase e-books instead of paperbacks. The question to those not yet initiated to the world of electronic reading is simply: *why?*

1. *Price.* An electronic title at Ellora's Cave Publishing and Cerridwen Press runs anywhere from 40-75% less than the cover price of the <u>exact same title</u> in paperback format. Why? Cold mathematics. It is less expensive to publish an e-book than it is to publish a paperback, so the savings are passed along to the consumer.

2. *Space.* Running out of room to house your paperback books? That is one worry you will never have with electronic novels. For a low one-time cost, you can purchase a handheld computer designed specifically for e-reading purposes. Many e-readers are larger than the average handheld, giving you plenty of screen room. Better yet, hundreds of titles can be stored within your new library—a single microchip. (Please note that Ellora's Cave and Cerridwen Press does not endorse any specific brands. You can check our website at www.ellorascave.com or

www.cerridwenpress.com for customer recommendations we make available to new consumers.)

3. *Mobility.* Because your new library now consists of only a microchip, your entire cache of books can be taken with you wherever you go.

4. *Personal preferences are accounted for.* Are the words you are currently reading too small? Too large? Too...**ANNOYING**? Paperback books cannot be modified according to personal preferences, but e-books can.

5. *Instant gratification.* Is it the middle of the night and all the bookstores are closed? Are you tired of waiting days—sometimes weeks—for online and offline bookstores to ship the novels you bought? Ellora's Cave Publishing sells instantaneous downloads 24 hours a day, 7 days a week, 365 days a year. Our e-book delivery system is 100% automated, meaning your order is filled as soon as you pay for it.

Those are a few of the top reasons why electronic novels are displacing paperbacks for many an avid reader. As always, Ellora's Cave and Cerridwen Press welcomes your questions and comments. We invite you to email us at service@ellorascave.com, service@cerridwenpress.com or write to us directly at: 1056 Home Ave. Akron OH 44310-3502.

erridwen, the Celtic Goddess of wisdom, was the muse who brought inspiration to storytellers and those in the creative arts. Cerridwen Press encompasses the best and most innovative stories in all genres of today's fiction. Visit our site and discover the newest titles by talented authors who still get inspired - much like the ancient storytellers did, once upon a time.

Cerridwen Press

www.cerridwenpress.com

MAKE EACH DAY MORE *EXCITING* WITH OUR

ELLORA'S CAVEMEN

CALENDAR

WWW.ELLORASCAVE.COM